THE Daffodils

Other Apple Paperbacks
you will enjoy:

Sticks and Stones, Bobbie Bones
by Brenda C. Roberts

Kate's Turn
by Jeanne Betancourt

Kool Ada
by Sheila Solomon Klass

Cousins
by Virginia Hamilton

Till's Christmas
by Nola Thacker

THE Daffodils

Christi Killien

AN
APPLE
PAPERBACK

SCHOLASTIC INC.
New York Toronto London Auckland Sydney

ISBN 0-590-44242-2

12 11 10 9 8 7 6 5 4   4 5 6 7 8/9

Printed in the U.S.A.   28

Contents

◇

THE Daffodils

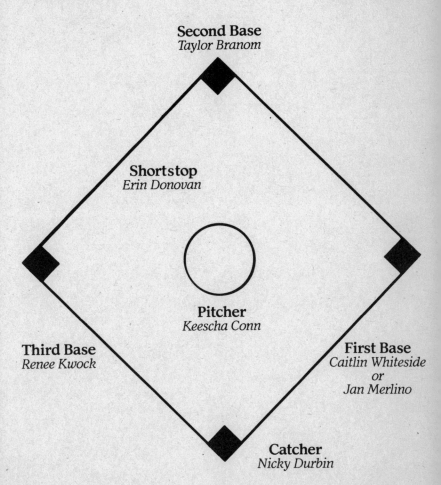

Center Field
Susan Ray

Left Field
Katie McMaster

Right Field
Jeannie Lehman

Second Base
Taylor Branom

Shortstop
Erin Donovan

Pitcher
Keescha Conn

Third Base
Renee Kwock

First Base
Caitlin Whiteside
or
Jan Merlino

Catcher
Nicky Durbin

The Daffodils

◇ 1 ◇
"We Are Number One!"

Nicole Durbin stopped at the Ordmore Elementary fence, tucked her hand into the smooth leather of her catcher's mitt, looked out on the newly chalked field where her team was warming up, and felt a moment of intense, wordless joy.

The keen smell of freshly mowed grass filled her nostrils. She chewed her good-luck Bubble Yum slowly, squishing the sweet, rubbery wad between her teeth. The Daffodils — sponsored by Elaine's Garden Center — were the champions of all Bainbridge Island last year, and Nicky couldn't wait to show the world that they would be again this year.

Nicky watched Coach Kwock in the distance as she dropped a big brown box against the fence. The new team T-shirts and caps, Nicky thought, feeling her heart pounding under the old T-shirt.

The Daffodil uniform was a yellow T-shirt, with black letters spelling DAFFODILS, and a yellow cap. Today was the first practice, and she, as last year's team captain, would get to hand them out. She touched the silver captain's whistle that hung around her neck.

Keescha Conn, the best player the Daffodils had and one of Nicky's best friends, stood tall on the pitcher's mound, throwing practice pitches to another Daffodil (Nicky couldn't tell who). Keescha's life goal was to be the first woman in the major leagues.

Jan Merlino and Erin Donovan leaned against the wooden backstop, talking. They kept looking past Nicky, in the direction of the parking lot.

Nicky could see a couple of Daffodils jogging out to the field to warm up. She kicked the fence and allowed herself a quiet "Yippeee!", then raced across the clumpy grass to her team.

"Hi, you guys!" she cried, waving.

Keescha stopped and looked across the diamond, her dark face seeming even darker against the background of sunlit alder trees beyond the fence. "Hey! Get your gear on, Nicky! I've got to practice some fastballs, and Jeannie's chicken."

So, it was Jeannie who Keescha had talked into practicing.

Jeannie Lehman stood up, her knees snapping so straight that she jumped in outrage. "Take that back," she shouted at Keescha, yanking the catcher's mask from her small freckled face. Jeannie was the youngest on the team — she had just turned ten in September. She was Nicky's other best friend besides Keescha.

"Lighten up," Keescha barked to Jeannie.

"Same to you!"

Nicky knew how to handle these disputes. She wasn't team captain for nothing. "Save your fast-balls for the Clippers," Nicky said, smiling. "I could hardly handle those balls last year. This year they'll burn my mitt."

Keescha grinned, and strolled to home plate. "Good 'ole Nicky," she said. "Smooth as butter."

Jeannie pushed her Daffodil cap way back on her head till it was nearly falling off. "See if I play with you again, Keescha," she said, scowling.

"Come on, Jeannie," Nicky said. "You know how Keescha is."

"Yeah, you know how I am." Keescha, still grinning, punched Jeannie playfully on the arm.

"A pain," Jeannie said, but she smiled at Keescha anyway.

"Lose that grin, kid," Keescha chided, reaching over to slap her glove on Jeannie's bottom. "You're ticked off, remember?"

"Keescha!" Jeannie cried.

Nicky stepped behind Jeannie and planted both her hands on Jeannie's narrow, bony shoulders. "March," she said. "Let's go see who is here this year, and get our new uniforms." Then, glancing at Keescha and pointing her index finger to the sky, Nicky and Keescha sang together, "We ARE Number One! We-Are-Number-One!"

When they got to the sideline, Jeannie plopped onto the bench and pouted. Keescha began to examine the stitching on the new softballs.

"Here, Nicky," Coach Kwock said, handing over her clipboard. "You can be interim captain until we vote later on in the week, okay?"

"Sure." Nicky was a little surprised that the coach even asked. Of course she'd be interim captain. Who else could?

Then she realized that the coach was trying to make everything fair. Nothing assumed. Coach Kwock had taught high school PE before she quit to raise her family. She was always careful to be fair.

"Put a check next to each girl you see who was on the team last year, and give them their new T-shirt." Coach Kwock pointed to the large cardboard box against the fence. "They can pull it on over their old shirt, if they want."

Keescha let out a piercing whistle. "Hear that, you guys," she said to Nicky and Jeannie, "no stripping on the field."

Nicky chuckled, but was too interested in the rest of the coach's instructions to joke around with Keescha. Jeannie looked puzzled. She hadn't gotten Keescha's joke.

"Never mind," Nicky said to Jeannie. Then, over Jeannie's shoulder, she noticed a couple of girls she'd never seen before and a grown-up walking slowly toward them. "What about the new members, Coach?" she asked.

Coach Kwock looked up. "Oh, yes, they must be Katie and Taylor. They're fifth-graders, too, but go to a private school. They ordered T-shirts just like everyone else." She pointed to the box. "I've marked the shirts already, Nicky. Look for pieces of masking tape with their names."

"Right," Nicky said.

"I'll be back in a minute." Coach Kwock moved toward the group, her hand extended.

◇ 5

Nicky propped one knee on the bench as a table for the clipboard.

She blew the whistle. "Roll call," she shouted. Then, to Jeannie, "Would you hand out the shirts when I call the names?"

Jeannie perked up. "Should I bring the box over here?" she asked.

"We can read," Keescha said. "Just let us get our own out of the box."

Nicky bristled at Keescha's interference, but, she told herself, a good team captain shouldn't be bossy for no reason. Do it Keescha's way. What was the difference? Probably Jeannie would need help, anyway. "Okay," she said, "but no crowding or pushing. Wait until the girl before you has found hers."

Jeannie nodded, her face solemn.

Keescha rolled her eyes. "Just get on with it. I'm here to play ball."

Nicky started calling out names. When the first Daffodil pulled her new shirt out of the box, someone groaned. "They're the same as last year's!"

"What did you expect, Erin?" Keescha said. "Daffodils are yellow."

Nicky looked up to see Erin glowering at Keescha. Erin had taken off her jacket and she wasn't wearing her old Daffodil T-shirt. Instead, she wore a black T-shirt with the rock group Hardboiled Egg written across it, and so did the new girl, Caitlin Whiteside, who stood beside her.

Caitlin had moved to Bainbridge Island from Seattle three weeks ago. Her long blonde hair was done in a French braid with pink ribbons laced throughout. The black T-shirt she wore now was actually a tank top, and her iridescent pink bra strap stuck out.

"Did you lose your old Daffodil T-shirt?" Nicky asked Erin. Nicky had a couple of extras if Erin needed one, to alternate.

"No. It's at home." Erin's eyes narrowed to slits. "I like this one better."

Nicky was startled.

"The Hardboiled Eggs are so cool," Caitlin chimed in. "I got these T-shirts free. I got to go backstage one time."

"So we've heard," Keescha said. Nicky had heard this, too. Caitlin kept saying how she knew all the members of the band, their birthdays, their favorite colors, their girlfriends. Nicky had stopped listening. Apparently the other girls hadn't.

Renee Kwock, the coach's daughter, peeked

over Erin's shoulder and added, "Caitlin's brother gave her the shirts. He works on the crew."

"Yeah," Jan said. "And Caitlin had a great idea for the team's T-shirts. Didn't she, Erin?"

"Ooo, yeah," Erin said. She smiled at Caitlin. "Can I tell?"

Caitlin shrugged. "Why not?" she said.

"They would be black, with one glittery yellow Daffodil on the front. No letters, just the symbol. Isn't that cool?" Erin beamed at Caitlin.

"Designer T-shirts," Keescha scoffed, pulling her new T-shirt from the box. "Give me a break."

"Not *designer*," Caitlin said, staring at Keescha. "Since Erin brought it up, I'll tell you. On my old team in Seattle, we had different shirts every year. Our coach drew a new design, then had it *silk-screened* onto specially dyed T-shirts."

Everyone was silent. Jeannie studied her sneakers.

"Not that you guys have to do it just like that," Caitlin added.

"What position did you play?" Keescha asked.

"First."

"Jan's our first base."

"We can share," Caitlin said, smiling at Jan.

"Yeah," said Jan.

Keescha said coolly, "That's up to the coach."

Erin folded her arms across her chest. "Well, I'm not going to wear this dumb yellow T-shirt."

Nicky's heart dropped into her stomach.

"Me, neither," Jan said.

"Hey, you guys," Nicky said, trying not to sound as desperate as she felt. Her mind raced with possible solutions. "You can always, uh, take your T-shirt to the mall and get some black daffodils pressed onto them."

"Yeah," Susan said, then looked at Caitlin.

Caitlin nodded. "It doesn't matter," she said, looking bored.

Nicky felt some relief and, hurriedly, finished the roll call and T-shirt distribution. She had forgotten how the first day or two of practice could be a little rough. Of course there would be a few disagreements, she thought. Everyone was nervous about defending the Daffodils' title as champs. There were new members to fit in, new positions to be assigned. Nothing that a little team spirit couldn't smooth out.

◇ 2 ◇
Good-Luck Gum

Jeannie's mother had to work, so Jeannie rode home with Nicky after practice. Nicky's father and her six-year-old sister, Emily, picked them up. Mr. Durbin taught math at Bainbridge High School, which was just next door to Ordmore Elementary and the middle school.

"How'd it go, girls?" Mr. Durbin asked.

"Great!" Nicky said. Once the initial squabbling was over, the players *had* been good. The coach even commented on the new talent.

"We've got three new players, and they're all pretty good, don't you think, Jeannie?"

"I guess." Jeannie's hair stuck up like tumbleweeds since she'd taken off her Daffodil cap.

"Taylor is the fastest runner on the team, I'll

bet you anything," Nicky continued. "And Caitlin can think fast. Did you see how she scooped up Jan's grounder, tagged first, and then threw the ball to Renee on third?"

"Yeah."

"There were some great plays, Dad."

Emily rode in the front seat. She turned around and said to Jeannie, "Did you bring your Barbie?"

Jeannie smiled and patted her backpack. "Right here. I got the prettiest new outfit for Easter. It's a ball gown that converts into a swimsuit."

Emily cooed in admiration.

"I got something for your Barbie, Nicky," Jeannie said softly, almost secretly, the way she talked when they first played together back in second grade.

Nicky's mother had died from cancer three years earlier, when Nicky was eight. Jeannie's parents were getting divorced then, and the two of them, Nicky and Jeannie, became friends. They had played dolls every afternoon.

They still played Barbies every once in a while, but right now, Nicky didn't want to talk about Barbies. She wanted to talk about the Daffodils. "Great, Jeannie. Show it to me when we get home, okay?"

But Jeannie was already unzipping her pack. She laid a Barbie softball uniform in Nicky's lap, complete with plastic bat, ball, and cleats. Nicky had seen it in the store a couple of months ago and wanted it.

Nicky smiled when she saw the small yellow piece of tape with DAFFODILS printed on it that Jeannie had made and stuck on the back of the little shirt. "I couldn't find a little whistle," Jeannie said.

"I've got a Barbie whistle!" Emily said. "It came with an aerobics outfit. You can have it, Nicky."

"This is neat, Jeannie." Nicky meant it. The outfit was a nice present, and it wasn't even her birthday. "Thanks. And thanks for the whistle, Em." Nicky wondered if it were on a silver chain like her real team captain's whistle.

Jeannie and Emily beamed like a pair of headlights.

"Hey, Dad?" Nicky said, noticing the HiHo grocery coming up. "Can we stop here for a second? I want to get some treats for practice tomorrow."

Mr. Durbin laughed and turned into the HiHo parking lot. "Nicky and her good-luck gum," he said.

"We're going to be unbeatable!" Nicky said.

* * *

The next afternoon, the infield smelled heavily of tutti-frutti Bubble Yum during the warm-up exercises, which Nicky helped lead. Twenty-five jumping jacks, ten toe-touches, and one lap around the field.

"Let's play," Coach Kwock announced when Jeannie finally jogged across the home plate after her lap. "I'll be rotating players today. Keescha, start as pitcher. Nicky, catcher. Caitlin, let's try you again at first. Taylor, second base; Renee, third; Erin, shortstop; Jeannie, right field; Susan, center field; Katie, left field; and Jan, you bat first."

The girls all clapped once, then scrambled for their mitts and ran out onto the field. Nicky strapped on her shinguards and chest pad. "Remember the signals?" she said to Keescha. Nicky had invented pitching signals for Keescha, even though all of her pitches were nearly the same. Some of the signals made them feel professional; others were just for fun.

"Do I remember!" Keescha flapped her hands next to her ears, Nicky's signal for "This person can hit anything; I have no idea what to tell you."

"I won't be giving you that signal our first game," Nicky said. "The coach told me we play the Clippers next week." The Clippers — sponsored by Gloria's Clip and Curl — were the worst team in the league.

"No problem," Keescha said and strode to the mound.

Jan walked to the plate and stood awkwardly. "Relax," Nicky whispered. "Slam it out there like yesterday."

Keescha pitched, and Jan swung late, as if her arms were strapped down.

The second pitch was wide, but Jan reached for it anyway.

"It's okay," Nicky soothed. "Third time's a charm."

Jan swung and connected, popping the ball out into center field. Susan Ray cried "Mine!", positioned herself under the ball, then let the ball spring off the tip of her mitt.

Keescha shook her head in disgust.

"Keep your eye on the ball, Susan," Coach Kwock called from the sideline. "Hold your mitt lower."

The rest of practice was more of the same. Batters swung with no energy, struck out, let themselves get tagged out, and fielders stumbled over balls and tufts of grass. Worst of all, no one was having fun.

"A bad day," Keescha commented to Nicky.

Nicky nodded. The team really needed her as captain this year, even more than last. She'd have to think of some new ways to get the players going. Starting with today.

Maybe the trouble had been the tutti-frutti. The smell *was* distracting. Tomorrow she would go back to straight strawberry.

◇3◇
The Vote

It was Thursday, the end of practice, and time for the team captain election. The sun hung low in the sky, the rays filtering through the alder trees, making zebras in the forest.

The Daffodils crowded around the bench.

Nicky clasped her hands behind her back to keep them from shaking.

"As you know, girls, today we elect our new team captain," Coach Kwock said. She looked tiny next to Keescha, who was six inches taller. "For those of you who weren't with us last year, the team captain's job is crucial." She glanced around at each of the girls. "The captain must be responsible and dedicated to the team. Please keep these qualities in mind when you make your nominations."

Nicky felt her face growing hot in the cool afternoon. She was embarrassed that the coach was so complimentary, but she couldn't help feeling, too, that Coach Kwock could have mentioned her by name.

"Are there any nominations?" the coach called out in an important voice.

Jeannie's hand shot up. "Nicky!" she said and grinned at her friend.

"Nicole Durbin has been nominated for a second year. Are there any other nominations?"

Nicky felt a pressure in her chest pushing its way to her mouth like soda in a capped bottle. Her hand went up. "Jeannie Lehman," she said. Nicky didn't want to seem conceited. A real election needed two candidates.

Coach Kwock frowned slightly. "Jeannie Lehman has been nominated. Is that all?"

Nicky was considering the coach's frown, that probably Jeannie would make a terrible captain since she was so quiet, when Erin raised her hand and announced, "I nominate Caitlin Whiteside."

"Caitlin?" Nicky said, snapping her head around to Caitlin, who stood at the end of the bench. Renee, Jan, Erin, Susan, and Taylor all seemed to be huddled around Caitlin like sticks of gum in a pack.

Caitlin pointed to herself and, acting surprised, said, "*Me?*"

"Caitlin Whiteside is our third nominee," the coach said. "Are there any others?"

The team stood in silence. Nicky clutched the team captain's whistle hanging around her neck. *Caitlin?* she kept thinking. No one even *knew* her.

"Okay, girls, here are your ballots and some pencils. Please write the name of your choice and fold the ballot. I'll collect them in a minute."

Nicky quickly wrote Jeannie's name on her ballot. It didn't seem right not to vote for the person you nominated. Then, as she waited for the coach to come by with the upturned cap, Nicky watched her friends.

None of the other girls besides Jeannie and Keescha would look her in the eye.

Erin voted for Caitlin, of course, Nicky thought, as she watched Erin drop her ballot into the coach's cap. Then, looking closely, Nicky realized that Erin was wearing lipstick. Caitlin's lipstick. When had Erin put it on? Nicky felt sure Erin's lips weren't purple at school. She would have noticed.

Susan squinted at Coach Kwock, who stood

directly in front of her. Susan wasn't wearing her glasses. Nicky wondered why. Last year, in the game against the Fenders — a team sponsored by Chuck Bender's Body and Fender — Susan's old glasses (which she hated) had flown from her face, had actually taken flight as she swatted a foul ball. Nicky, as catcher, had almost stepped on them. "Please, Nicky," Susan had begged while everyone else watched the ball sail into the bleachers. "Really crunch them, okay?" Nicky had obliged. Susan had gotten neat, big-frame glasses the next week. Where were they now?

And, Nicky blinked in disbelief, but it was true: Jan Merlino, who was standing next to Susan, had just tugged at the bottom of what could only be a bra. It was either that, or some sort of back brace. Jan wouldn't meet Nicky's eyes, even though Nicky looked straight at her.

Nicky's stomach began to ache. *What if she lost?* It was unthinkable.

Jeannie grinned at Nicky unconcernedly as the entire team waited while Coach Kwock tallied the ballots.

"Come *on*," Keescha muttered from beside Nicky.

Nicky stood as straight as the baseball bat propped against the bench beside her.

"Listen up, girls," Coach Kwock said, shoving the ballots back into the hat and picking up her tally sheet. "It was very close, but we do have a winner."

All of the girls breathed in at once.

Nicky stood absolutely still, her hat pulled low, her catcher's mitt tucked under her arm. She was a human monument to perfect posture and attentiveness as she waited to hear the results.

"Caitlin Whiteside, congratulations!" the coach announced with a big smile.

"Yeah!" Jan, Susan, Erin, and Renee all cried, leaping up and down around Caitlin and squealing.

Nicky felt her heart shrink into a golf ball, small and hard.

Jeannie and Keescha both looked at Nicky. Nicky knew they wanted to see what she would do. Nicky didn't know what she could do besides look like she felt nothing. *Her team hadn't re-elected her.*

"Now, now," Coach Kwock said, glancing around at the cheering girls, giving her daughter an unusually hard look, and then, finally, stopping at Nicky. "As I said, it was close, and I'm sure Nicky will be a big help to Caitlin if she has any questions. Nicky, I want to thank you publicly for the fine job you did for us last year."

Nicky willed the tears forming in the back of her eyes to retreat. She would not cry. She wouldn't look like a baby.

What good were the coach's words *now*? she thought, mustering herself. Coach Kwock wanted her to help Caitlin! What help did *she* need?

The coach continued. "Caitlin," she said, "Nicole Durbin did an outstanding job last year. She organized the equipment in a way that can only be described as brilliant. I think Nicky's biggest contribution was the colored tape on the bats showing the number of hits a girl got with that particular bat." She smiled broadly at Nicky. Nicky tried to smile, to be a good sport, but her lips seemed to be twitching uncontrollably.

The most awful moment was yet to come, though, and she had to endure it with dignity.

"Let's have a round of applause for Nicky!" Coach Kwock cried.

Keescha and Jeannie whooped it up — Keescha punched her fist in the air, and Jeannie whistled — while the other girls, including the purple-lipped Erin, blinded Susan, and bra-bound Jan, clapped politely, as if they had all just polished their nails.

"Thank you," Coach Kwock said. "Nicky, do you have the whistle?"

Nicky removed the whistle from around her neck. The sun came out from behind a cloud at that moment, and the whistle gleamed in her hand. The moment was still, caught in slow motion, and her arms moved heavily, the way they did in her nightmares when a player was stealing second base.

She walked over to Caitlin. Caitlin stepped forward, and Nicky reached out to hand over the whistle. Her hand bumped Caitlin's, though, and the whistle dropped to the ground. Caitlin waited. Nicky waited. Caitlin was going to make her pick it up!

Hastily Nicky bent over to get it, and in that moment she saw Caitlin's exaggerated shadow cast on the dirt above the whistle. For a moment, it was the shadow of a *teenager*, the curve of her peaked chest outlined clearly in the circle of chain lying in the dirt. The swollen shadow adjusted its bra, and Nicky looked up. Was this really eleven-year-old Caitlin's shadow? Nicky continued to look up. Caitlin grinned down at Nicky and smoothed her pearly lipstick with her pinkie. "Thanks," Caitlin said.

"See you on Saturday, girls," the coach said and clapped her hands once.

Nicky, Keescha, and Jeannie watched as Caitlin walked away with half of the Daffodils trailing after her.

◇4◇
Sorry, But . . .

"The whole team used to leave together," Jeannie said softly.

Nicky pulled her cap down lower over her forehead to keep her emotions in place, and started walking with her two friends across the field to the waiting cars. Caitlin and her crowd walked a distance in front of them.

"I can't believe it," Keescha said loudly. "Caitlin knows zip about the team."

Jeannie nodded as she walked. "It's not fair," she said. She reached up and patted Nicky on the shoulder.

Nicky said nothing, but picked up her pace. They arrived at the parking area in silence. Keescha scowled at Caitlin, who was leaning against a tree. Only Jan and Erin stood next to her now, but they were too far away for Nicky to hear their conversation.

"Guess who I am," Keescha said suddenly. She stuck out her chest and began to prance around in a circle, patting her tight, curly hair. "Eeeee!" she screamed and pointed at a dumpster. *"Boys!"*

Jeannie and Nicky laughed. Jan, Erin, and Caitlin looked over and shook their heads. Erin curled her purple lips in disgust.

A teenage boy drove up at that moment in his rusty yellow pickup truck. "Lookin' good there!" he called out, eyeing Keescha.

Keescha stopped, and Jeannie ducked behind Nicky. "Who asked you?" Keescha yelled back, planting her hands on her hips.

"Hoooo-wee!" the boy hooted and covered his head with his arms. "Listen to that mouth!"

"Get lost," Keescha called, punching her fist at him.

The boy laughed harder.

Nicky wished her father would get there, but even more than that, she wished Keescha would just ignore the guy.

"Leave her alone, Caleb," Caitlin said, strutting over to the truck and climbing in.

"I can take care of myself, Miss Caitlin,"

Keescha muttered and flipped her hand in the air.

"Bye, Erin! Bye, Jan!" Caitlin cried from the truck and waved.

"Bye!" Erin and Jan sang back in unison.

Caleb roared the engine. The yellow truck jerked backward. He ground the gearshift for a moment, then the truck lurched forward and sped away in a cloud of dust.

"Turkey!" Keescha yelled out.

Jan and Erin stared at Keescha.

Keescha called, "Who was *that*?" and stomped over to the two girls. Nicky followed slowly with Jeannie. Nicky wasn't sure she could face Jan and Erin so soon after the election.

Jan twisted to look for her parents' car, then had to pull her bra down. "My mom is *late*," she said and rolled her eyes.

"Who was that?" Keescha repeated.

"Who?" Jan said.

"That guy who hooted at me."

"Oh, that's Caitlin's brother. He travels — "

"Don't tell me about that stupid rock group again," Keescha snapped.

"Caitlin is really nice," said Erin, planting her hand on her hip and glaring at Keescha. "Not like some people I know."

Then, looking over at Nicky, Erin added in

a softer voice, "Sorry about the election, Nicky, but you've already been captain. And Caitlin's really nice. You'll like her, too, once you get to know her."

Nicky couldn't meet Erin's eyes. Her heart was breaking, shattering into a thousand pieces, and no one seemed to realize that.

"Yeah," said Jan. "Caitlin gave Erin that lipstick. Isn't it pretty?"

Nicky could see Keescha starting to laugh, so she forced herself to answer. It was a relief to change the subject, to show everyone that she wasn't devastated. "I was wondering about that lipstick," she said to Erin. Nicky smiled as best she could. "You didn't have it on at school."

"It's grape," Erin said and giggled. "I ate it all off three times during practice!"

Nicky stretched her own lips in a wider smile. But she was thinking, no wonder three runners whizzed to third base untagged.

"Caitlin's bringing me a peach one tomorrow," said Jan. "She's got tons of them. Maybe she'll bring one for you, Nicky, if you ask her."

"Gro — " Keescha began, but Nicky interrupted. "See you guys tomorrow. Come on, Keescha. Your dad just drove up." She started walking away.

"Bye, Nicky," Erin and Jan said.

Keescha followed Nicky, but dragged her feet. "Erin's lips looked like they had been turned inside out," she scoffed.

"Why were you so nice to them?" Jeannie asked Nicky. "You know they voted for Caitlin."

Nicky shrugged. "It's over," Nicky said, feeling the pain of the loss clamping its grip tighter around her chest. "There's your mom," she said to Jeannie, changing the subject again.

Jeannie stopped and looked up at Nicky. Softly, she said, "Maybe we can play later, okay?"

Nicky knew she meant dolls, but for some reason, neither one of them said the word.

"Yeah, maybe," Nicky said. "See you later."

Nicky and Keescha watched Jeannie climb into her mom's old blue car.

"You're still captain as far as I'm concerned," Keescha said suddenly.

"Thanks," Nicky said.

A honk came from Keescha's father's gray Dodge. "I gotta go," Keescha said, suddenly nervous. Nicky knew Keescha's father was strict, and she had better get going when he honked.

"Go on," Nicky said. She saw her own father pulling into a parking space at the end of the row. "See ya tomorrow," she said to Keescha.

Nicky jogged down to her car, wiping frantically at the tears that suddenly pooled in her eyes when she saw her family. They were smiling and waving at her.

◇ 5 ◇
"I Don't Want
to Talk About It"

"Hi!" Nicky said when she got to the car. She didn't look at Emily or her father. She felt Emily staring at her from the backseat, though.

"Where's your whistle?" Emily asked. She leaned over Nicky's shoulder to see the front of her T-shirt again.

Nicky turned and gazed at her sister. "I gave it to the new team captain," she said matter-of-factly.

Emily frowned. "You mean you aren't team captain anymore?"

"I've already had a year of team captain, Emily. It's only fair that someone else get a turn."

"Oh," Emily said, glancing at Mr. Durbin, then dropping into her seat.

Nicky swung back around and fastened her seatbelt. Mr. Durbin hadn't started the car yet. He was watching Nicky, but Nicky locked her eyes in place along with her seatbelt, keeping her true feelings safe.

"Hmmm," Mr. Durbin said. "Well." He started the engine, and the radio popped to life with the news.

Nicky pretended to be listening. She could see her father's lap, his long foot pressing the gas pedal, his hands on the steering wheel as he drove, but she couldn't look at his face.

When Mr. Durbin pulled into the driveway, Jeannie was riding up on her bike. She had her Barbie box propped on her handlebars.

"Jeannie!" Emily cried out her window. "Did you bring that gown you told us about?"

Jeannie waved and patted the box.

"Thanks for picking me up, Dad," Nicky said over her shoulder as she hopped out of the car. She looked at the top of his balding head, not at his face.

Actually, she felt glad to see Jeannie and her Barbie dolls. They were a perfect excuse not to linger near her father.

Emily ran ahead into the house.

"I'm *really* mad about you losing team captain," Jeannie said to Nicky as they climbed the stairs to Nicky's room. "Caitlin thinks she is so tough."

"I don't want to talk about it, Jeannie, okay?"

Jeannie paused a moment, then said, "You know, Nicky, I know what you mean. I don't want to talk about Fritz, either."

Nicky looked at her friend, suddenly confused. What did Jeannie's older brother have to do with losing the team captainship?

"You don't want to talk about Caitlin, I don't want to talk about Fritz," Jeannie explained with a flip of her hand.

"If you mean because Fritz teases you, it's not the same," Nicky said in an even voice. "Caitlin hasn't said anything to me personally. There's just nothing more to talk about."

"Yeah, I guess." They were at Nicky's door now. "I'll go set up the Barbies," Jeannie said.

Nicky ducked into the bathroom and glanced at herself in the mirror. Yes, she looked the same. At least nothing noticeable had changed. Same black hair, straight-across bangs, blue eyes. Nothing had changed, really.

She crossed the hall to her room. Emily was there now, and had looped her Barbie whistle around Nicky's Barbie's neck. She held it up as Nicky walked in. "Look! Isn't it perfect?"

"Emily, I told you, I'm not the team captain anymore!" Nicky shouted.

Emily's mouth fell open.

"That doesn't mean you can't *play* like you're still captain," Jeannie said.

"Yes, it does! Like I said to Emily in the car, I had my turn last year. The team wants *Caitlin*. Who's to say the Daffodils won't be just as good with her? The least we can do is give her a chance."

Nicky looked down at Jeannie and Emily on the floor. Neither of them even tried to refute Nicky's words.

If Keescha had been there, Nicky thought, she would have argued with Nicky, called her good sportsmanship baloney, and insisted that Caitlin had won a popularity contest, all of which Nicky wouldn't have minded hearing.

"Let's just play," she said resolutely and sat down, feeling as hollow as the Barbie dolls. For the rest of the afternoon, she kept her feelings small.

She still felt empty from her speech when she went to bed that night. She was sick of being the graceful loser. She wished she had voted for herself. Had her vote for Jeannie made the difference? It could have, Nicky calculated, lying there in her bed. It depended on Katie's and Taylor's votes, and if Caitlin voted for herself.

Mr. Durbin knocked on her door, then walked in and sat quietly on the edge of her bed. He waited.

"It's hard to talk about it," she said. Her throat was dry. "I can still hardly believe it."

"I know the feeling."

Nicky remembered how he hadn't talked much, at first, after her mother had died. He'd go to bed early or work by himself in the garage. Nicky didn't know if that was what her father was thinking of. It seemed wrong, somehow, to compare losing team captain to a death, but that's what it felt like to Nicky.

"Remember when I started playing softball last year?" Nicky said. "You came to all my games?" Tears started to pool, but she didn't care.

"I will again this year," said Mr. Durbin gently. "You know that, don't you?"

"I know it," Nicky said, allowing tears to trickle down her cheeks, "but I feel so sad about losing that. . . ." She stopped to swallow and to wipe her eyes. "Are you disappointed with me?"

Mr. Durbin reached over and held her face in his palms. "I like to watch *you*. It doesn't matter if you're captain or not." His eyes watered now. "It doesn't even matter if you're playing softball. Watching you pour a glass of milk makes me happy."

Nicky shook her head. Sadness stuck in her throat, thick and dry, like a hot dog bun. She had been holding her arms tightly, and now she let them go limp. "Why didn't they vote for me?" she cried into her father's shoulder.

He didn't have an answer, and neither did she.

◇ 6 ◇
Caitlin

The next day, Nicky, Keescha, and Jeannie had finished their lunches and were walking out to recess. The day was cloudy and cool, with fog still misting the corners of the playground.

"There she is," Nicky said to her friends. She watched Caitlin as she stood in the middle of a pack of girls near the monkey bars. She wore the team captain's whistle, as well as nylon stockings (with a hole in the right knee) and dangly earrings.

"Who are you talking about?" Keescha said, reaching up and swatting a tetherball.

"Caitlin," said Nicky. No one seemed to remember yesterday's election except Nicky.

"Caitlin's a scab," said Keescha. "Ignore her, and she'll go away."

Jeannie laughed. She pulled a broken piece of chain bracelet out of her pocket, her hopscotch marker. "Want to play?" she asked Keescha.

"Naw," Keescha said. "I want to play tetherball." She pounded the tetherball again, ducking as it whipped around the pole. "Come on, Nicky."

Nicky and Keescha had first become friends playing tetherball. Nicky was the only kid besides Justin (who was the tallest kid in their class) who could beat Keescha. Every time they played, a crowd gathered to watch.

"Okay," Nicky said.

"My serve," Keescha was saying when Greg Gibbons ran by, practically knocking Nicky down.

"Watch it!" Keescha yelled at him.

Nicky saw him race by Caitlin and snap her bra strap. Caitlin screamed. The girls around her, including Jan, Erin, and Susan, dissolved into giggles. Some of the boys, including Jeffrey Barnett — the boy everyone said liked Nicky, but whom Nicky couldn't stand — stared at this activity just as Nicky, Keescha, and Jeannie did. They looked stunned, too.

"Did you see that?" Nicky said, not sure if she could trust her own eyes.

"If one of those boys did that to me, I'd feed his liver to my dog," Keescha remarked. She had gotten a bra long before Caitlin ever came on the scene — her mother gave it to her for Christmas. After wearing it one time, she had told Nicky that she would *never* wear it again. No one had paid the slightest bit of attention to Keescha's bra, however, which had been fine with Keescha.

Keescha continued to glare at Caitlin. "The girl is a ditz," she said. "I don't know why she's getting all this attention."

"Me, neither," Nicky said. Nicky rested one foot on a balance beam. She brushed her dark bangs off her forehead and continued to watch Caitlin.

"Yeah," said Jeannie, glowering. She brushed her reddish-blonde hair aside the exact way Nicky had. "Yeah."

"Yeah, *what*?" Keescha snapped, startling Jeannie.

"Never mind," Nicky said to Keescha. "Let's play."

Nicky stole glimpses of Caitlin between tetherball games. She didn't think Keescha was right about Caitlin being a ditz. Caitlin seemed smart, and she seemed to know exactly what she was doing.

No one watched Keescha and Nicky play tetherball that day except Jeannie.

On Mondays and Tuesdays, the fifth-graders got the softball field for morning recess. The teams were mixed, girls and boys, and Nicky was always one of the first chosen for the teams. It was Monday, and Nicky raced out the classroom door when the bell rang.

This is a great time to get in some extra practice, she was thinking as she ran down the asphalt path alongside the school, under the pussy willow tree, past a clump of blooming daffodils, and out across the wet, morning grass. Keescha ran beside her, as well as a couple of other girls and all of the fifth-grade boys.

"Come on, Renee!" Nicky bellowed when they started choosing up teams. Keescha and Justin were the captains. "Susan! Erin! Hurry up!"

"We aren't playing!" Jan cried back. The group of them stood around the slide, which was halfway between the field and the blacktop. Caitlin sat on the slide itself.

"Wait a second, you guys," Nicky said to Keescha, who had just picked Greg for her team. Greg was a strong batter.

"Tell them to get their butts over here," Keescha instructed.

Nicky jogged over. "We've got a game on Wednesday, you guys!" she said to her friends.

"We're going to watch," Caitlin said.

"Yeah," Jan said.

"Caitlin's going to watch *Greg*," Erin said and laughed.

"But we need this practice," Nicky said. She looked at Caitlin, hoping she'd see her point. As team captain, she should be setting an example.

"We practice every afternoon," Caitlin said, eyeing Nicky coolly. "That's enough. We want to talk."

"But — "

"ARE YOU PLAYING, NICKY?" Greg shouted.

Nicky turned. The teams were chosen and ready to play.

"Go and play," Caitlin said. Something in the way Caitlin said that, especially the word *play*, sounded sour.

The girls around Caitlin giggled.

Nicky felt her face begin to burn with embarrassment. This seemed to be exactly the reaction Caitlin wanted, because she smiled broadly at Nicky. "Greg's calling you," she added.

Nicky's mind raced, searching frantically for some remark, some dignified, cool response.

"NICKY!" Keescha cried.

Nicky turned and ran back to the softball field.

Erin, Jan, and Caitlin wore their Daffodil T-shirts to the Clipper game two days later, but Nicky hardly recognized them as the shirts she had handed out a week and a half ago.

They hadn't gotten stickers as Nicky suggested. Instead, Caitlin, Erin, and Jan had tie-dyed their T-shirts. Explosions of pink and blue covered the yellow material.

"Neat!" Renee and Susan cried.

"I love it!" said Taylor, who was spending more time now with Renee than she was with her friend Katie.

"We don't look like a team anymore," Nicky complained to Jeannie and Keescha.

"Who cares?" Keescha said. "Just as long as we play like one."

Jeannie didn't seem sympathetic, either. She just shrugged and tucked her shirt further down into her jeans. She was the only one who had her shirt tucked in, Nicky noticed. Nicky wanted to reach over and pull it out.

Coach Kwock frowned. She clapped and called the Daffodils together. "We don't exactly look like a team anymore," she said with a strained smile, and looked at Caitlin.

Caitlin didn't flinch. "We just wanted to make them pretty," she said.

A woman suddenly walked up and stood behind Caitlin. She was short, had curly brown hair, and dark circles under her eyes. "Caitlin said it would be all right," the woman said in a worried voice.

"*Mom*," Caitlin said.

"You're Caitlin's mother?" Coach Kwock asked.

"Yes." The woman smiled, then shrugged. "Should we have asked you?"

"Actually, that would have been best," the coach said.

"It was *Caleb's* idea," Caitlin whined.

"I'm so sorry," said Caitlin's mother.

Nicky knew without a doubt, looking at Caitlin's pouting face, that *Caitlin* wasn't sorry.

"It's done," the coach said. "Let's just get on with the game."

"I'm sorry," Caitlin's mother said again and hurried to the bleachers.

Caitlin rolled her eyes at Erin and Jan. Nicky couldn't believe that Caitlin would act so rude toward her mother in front of the entire team.

Coach Kwock clapped to get the team's attention. "We've got a game to play," she said and pointed with her clipboard to the blue-shirted Clippers who were just now arriving, running up the asphalt path from the parking lot and shouting like attack dogs. "Here they come."

The Clippers were a different team, Nicky could tell from watching their warm-up. "They've got a new pitcher," Nicky said to Jan and Erin. "She's good. I saw her playing at the park a couple weeks ago. I didn't know she was a Clipper then."

Erin shrugged. "Don't worry," she said, trading a lipstick with Jan.

"But, make sure you don't hit — " Nicky began when Jan interrupted her. *"Don't worry, Nicky."*

Nicky watched her apply a new coat of grape-smelling lipstick.

Keescha pitched her best game ever, striking out ten girls and catching two pop flies and a line-drive, but she couldn't play for the entire team. By the bottom of the seventh inning, the last inning of the game, the Daffodils were at bat, and the Clippers were ahead by two runs. The score was 21 to 19. The Daffodils were down, but they weren't out.

"HEADS UP, KATIE!" Nicky called from the bench as Katie stepped up to the plate. Katie waved to her mother in the bleachers.

"Come on, Slugger!" Keescha cried.

"Watch the ball, Katie," said Coach Kwock.

Katie stood straight at the plate. Someone should talk with Katie about her stance, Nicky thought. She looked at Caitlin, but Caitlin was talking with Erin and wasn't even watching the game.

The Clipper's pitcher aimed and threw. Katie swung, and the ball bobbled across the few feet of bumpy grass to the pitcher, who scooped it up and tossed it to the first baseman.

"One away," the umpire called.

Jan stepped up to the plate and pulled up her socks. "COME ON, JAN!" Nicky cheered.

Jan tugged at her underwear.

Then she pulled down her bra.

Finally, she stopped adjusting herself and bent over the plate, holding the bat at an awkwardly low angle. Nicky could see that if she held it higher, she'd nudge all of her elastic out of line.

Jan swung at the first pitch. *Whoosh.* She swung before the ball left the pitcher's hand.

The pitcher waited while Jan yanked her socks, her underwear, and her bra. In that order. Again.

Whoosh. Nicky sat helpless. Jan wasn't this bad last year. She wasn't concentrating.

"Make her give you a good one!" Keescha cried.

Jan swung so hard at the third pitch that she fell off balance. The Clippers' catcher caught *Jan* instead of the ball. Caitlin, who stood in the batter's circle, doubled over into hysterics. Jan looked hurt, but Caitlin patted her on the shoulder as she walked by. "No big deal!" Caitlin said.

Jan laughed then, too, though not very loudly. She passed Nicky on the way to the bench and shrugged. "No big deal," she repeated.

Nicky bit her lip. Caitlin's big grin made Nicky furious. Striking out right now *was* a big deal, she thought. There was only one out left! How could they win if every strike out was *no big deal*? Nicky didn't want to hurt Jan's feelings, though.

This was all Caitlin's fault. Jan wouldn't have been distracted by a bra if it weren't for Caitlin.

"Get some new socks," Keescha said to Jan,

who now sat next to her on the bench.

"Two away!" the umpire yelled, and swept off the plate.

Now Caitlin was at bat. Caitlin bent over the plate, the pitcher threw, and Caitlin connected. The ball sailed out over the second baseman into center field. The entire Daffodil bench held its breath, praying for the girl to miss the ball.

But she caught it, or at least it landed in her glove. She kept looking to make sure it was there. She was probably as surprised as everyone else.

"YOU'RE OUT!"

Caitlin hadn't even started her run to first base. "Oh, well," she said and laughed again.

"Blast," Keescha said, slamming her glove onto the ground. "That outfielder didn't even know she'd caught the ball!"

Nicky didn't care about the details of the catch. She cared that Caitlin hadn't run like crazy to first base. She cared that Caitlin had laughed, again. She cared that Caitlin didn't seem to care.

Later, when Nicky sang TWO, FOUR, SIX, EIGHT, WHO DO WE AP-PRE-CI-ATE? to the winning Clippers, she was still acting like a graceful loser.

She acted like a graceful loser, too, when her

father told her what a good game she had played. "We'll get 'em next time," she said.

But she wasn't thinking like a graceful loser anymore. She was thinking about how to win back the respect and allegiance of all the Daffodils and set the team up for another victorious season.

◇ 7 ◇

It's What's Upstairs
That Counts

"Dad?" Nicky said very sweetly.

Mr. Durbin was reading the newspaper. A stack of school papers lay on the coffee table in front of him, along with his red fake-leather grade book. He grunted, but did not lower the Living Section.

"Dad, I need to ask you something." She could see the few dark hairs from the top of his balding head sticking up behind the page.

"Mmm. Okay. Where's Emily?" he asked.

"Outside swinging."

"Mmmm." He turned the page.

"Dad, I need a bra."

Slowly the paper came down so that Nicky could see her father's forehead and glasses, but not his whole face. "A what?" she heard him say. His eyes looked sort of panicky, darting from one corner of the room to the other.

"A bra," she repeated.

Mr. Durbin cleared his throat and dropped the paper into his lap. Nicky thought his lip twitched. "Ah, a brassiere. Well. Uh. So, is it time for this already?" He seemed to be looking, intermittently, at Nicky's chest. She crossed her arms.

"Yes, it is time," she said positively. The Daffodils were splitting up, playing terribly. It was up to Nicky to keep them together. She had to be back in charge, had to win Jan and Erin and Susan over, and if that meant wearing a stupid bra like them, so be it.

"You're only eleven years old, Nicky."

"Age isn't the issue, Dad," Nicky said. She was prepared for this, and had thought out her arguments. "It's what's upstairs that counts."

Mr. Durbin looked at the ceiling. "Upstairs? What are you talking about now?"

Nicky pointed to her chest.

Her father smiled. *"That's* upstairs?"

Nicky nodded.

Her father cleared his throat again and then twisted his mouth to the side, the way he did to keep from laughing. "Oh. Well, I thought upstairs, when referring to the human body, meant the *head*."

"Not at my school," Nicky said and flushed. Her mind raced to remember how she had heard the word used. Could it have meant the head?

"Anyway," she continued, "I really need one, Dad."

Mr. Durbin sat forward and adjusted his glasses. "Nicky, honey, I don't know about this. Obviously I want to do the right thing here, but, well, I never had any sisters, you know. You seem a little young." He rubbed his hand across his chin. "Maybe I should call your grandma. She can talk with you about this."

Nicky cringed. Grandma Rose would have her in undershirts until ninth grade. "No, Dad. We can work this out ourselves, okay?"

"Well, maybe. Nicky, do you really *need* a brassiere?" Nicky watched as his face turned red.

"Dad, please. Call it a bra. No one calls it a brassiere."

"Oh, yes. Well, a bra, then. I don't know — "

"If you must know," Nicky interrupted, feeling a little flustered herself, "I bounce." The truth was that she bounced, or rather *jiggled*, only the merest bit every once in a while when she was jumping rope or playing hopscotch, but she couldn't tell her father that she wanted a bra because Caitlin and Jan (and probably Erin, too) had one. Everyone knew that that was the weakest argument ever made to a parent.

"Bounce?" said Mr. Durbin, puzzling out Nicky's meaning.

"*Yes*. My chest *bounces*. And about my age, Dad, no offense, but that doesn't make any sense. It's like glasses. Can I only get glasses when I'm a certain age?"

Nicky's father just looked at her. "Go on," he said.

"Of course not," Nicky said, gently slapping her palm on the coffee table. She felt good about this comparison. It was a powerful argument, she thought. "A person gets glasses when she needs them. And it's the same with bras." Nicky sat down in the chair opposite her father and looked straight at him.

"I agree," her father said.

Nicky willed herself to appear calm and in control. She was winning! "Then you can't say I'm too young for a bra," she said.

"Okay. Perhaps I should have said that you don't need one."

"Dad, how do *you* know? I'm sorry, but you don't know what it's like to be a *girl*."

He sighed deeply. "Nicky, getting a bra was

the furthest thing from your mind last week. Remember? You were working so hard on your batting, begging your sister to pitch to you. You were racing up and down the street with Jeannie, playing hide-and-seek or whatever that game is called, until eight o'clock. Wasn't that just last week?"

"Kick-the-can," Nicky corrected. "Hide-and-seek is for babies. And I was bouncing the whole time."

The truth? Nicky jiggled twice — when she jumped over the Hendersteins' fence, and when she was the last one in and won and hopped all over in a little victory dance.

"Mm." Mr. Durbin reached over and arranged his ungraded stack of papers. "I didn't notice any change in your all-out, wild running style, but, for the sake of argument, if you want to buy a bra and wear it when you play kick-the-can, I suppose that would be okay."

A bubble of joy rose in Nicky's flat chest. "And to school, too," she said.

"Uh, I don't know." He shifted uncomfortably in his worn maroon chair.

Nicky could see the agony her father was in. His face was creased into such a frown, it looked as if a boulder were pressing on his head, forcing his forehead and eyes into wrinkles of pain. But she had to get this bra. "Dad, we play kick-the-can at school, too!" she argued.

"*All right,*" he said and groaned.

"Can we go tomorrow?"

"You and *me?*" The way he said this, Nicky knew that shopping together would be too much. And, she suddenly realized, he probably shouldn't be allowed to see her chest ever again. She *was* developing, after all.

"Maybe I can ask Claire to take you," her father said suddenly. Claire, otherwise known as Mrs. Fishman, taught science across the hall from Nicky's dad. She was a good friend of his.

"Thanks, Dad," Nicky said, then added, "The sooner the better, you know?"

Her father turned pink again, but Nicky wasn't paying any attention. She was thinking of the Daffodils' game next week against the Fenders. Nicky wanted to play that game in a bra.

"I'll ask her tomorrow," Mr. Durbin said.

Nicky went up to her room while her father called Emily in for her bath. "Emily," Nicky could hear him call, feebly, from the kitchen door. He sounded exhausted.

As she climbed the steps, Nicky thought of the word *brassiere* again. She shuddered. It was the word for the huge elastic-and-wire things her grandmother had hanging in her bathroom all the time.

She stopped abruptly at her bedroom doorway, not going in. This entire discussion had made her hungry. She turned and bounded back down the stairs to get something to eat, and met Emily coming up.

"I can do a front hip circle on the bar!" Emily sang out.

"Wonderful."

"Do you want to see me?"

"You have to take your bath, and I have important plans to make."

"Tomorrow?" Emily begged.

"Emily, tomorrow I could be at the store getting a bra." Nicky let the enormity of this news sink in. Her sister's eyes grew satisfyingly large.

"A bra?" Emily repeated.

"That's what I said. A bra."

"What's a bra?"

Nicky let out a huge sigh of disgust. At times like this, she really missed having her mom around. It was up to Nicky to do all this stuff. "You must be joking," Nicky said.

Emily just stared.

"It's what girls wear when their breasts grow," Nicky said, "to keep them from bouncing."

"Oh."

"Go take your bath," Nicky said.

"Okay," Emily said, untying her shoes right there in the hall. "Maybe we can play the next day."

"Maybe." As Nicky plodded the rest of the way down the stairs, she couldn't help feeling a little sad about not playing on the bars and batting with Emily tomorrow afternoon. Was *she* ready for this bra business? What was she getting herself into?

◇ 8 ◇
Forcing
the Daffodils

Nicky put the second part of her plan into action the next day at recess. The playground swarmed with kids, and the cool, clear late April sky was full of screeching sea gulls.

Jeffrey and his friends were playing tetherball, but Jeffrey kept watching Nicky. Nicky ignored him. She sat with Jeannie on the balance beam while Keescha shot baskets.

"Did you see Caitlin passing those notes this morning?" Nicky asked her friends. Caitlin was safely out of earshot, hanging around the monkey bars and talking. As usual.

"What notes?" Jeannie asked.

"Notes to Erin and Jan," Nicky said.

"I thought she was just giving them lipstick," said Jeannie.

"Caitlin wants to take over everything," Nicky said.

"Who cares?" Keescha scoffed. She stopped her dribbling. "What's there for her to take over? Who needs her?"

"I don't care about *Caitlin*," Nicky said. "No matter what Jan and Erin say, I don't like her. *But*, I don't want her ruining our team, either."

"Me, neither!" Jeannie said.

"How is she going to ruin the team?" Keescha asked. "She's team captain, not the *coach*."

"She's already started!" Nicky cried. She spread her arms, taking in the entire playground. "Look how divided we are! There are Jan and Susan and Erin all gathered around her, whispering! We never did that before. We're split."

Nicky let them look around, then asked, "What happened to our tetherball tournaments and four-square matches? It seems like all the team has done out here for the past week is *talk*."

Jeannie looked up then. "I *know*," she said. "I hate it."

"So what do you think you can do about it?" Keescha said to Nicky.

"Fight fire with fire," Nicky said to Keescha. "Win those friends back!"

"How?" Keescha asked. She held the basketball against her hip.

This was what Nicky had been waiting for. "There's no going back," she said evenly. "Nobody's going to just stop wearing a bra, you know what I mean?"

"It would look like you never needed one," Jeannie said.

Keescha scowled, but Nicky continued. "Right. So, in order to get the team back together, I'm going to start wearing a bra." Nicky flushed with the revelation.

Jeannie gasped.

Keescha said in a hard, accusing voice, "That's stupid."

Nicky was flustered at first, then nudged her anger to the surface and glared at Keescha. "Can you think of another way to get Jan and Susan and Erin back over here with us?" Nicky looked at each of her friends carefully, then, lowering her voice, continued. "We've got to win back the other girls on the team."

"That's" the reason you're getting a bra?" Keescha blurted. "How does that make you any different from Caitlin?"

Nicky was hurt momentarily, but Jeannie frowned. "Whose side are you on?" Jeannie said to Keescha. "Nicky's not like Caitlin!"

Nicky had a revelation. "No offense, Jeannie, but Keescha's right," Nicky said. "I don't want sides. That's the whole point!"

Jeannie's freckled cheeks grew bright red, as if Nicky had just slapped her.

"I shouldn't have said fire with fire," Nicky explained. "What I *meant* was if you can't beat 'em, join 'em. We'll be one team again!" Nicky smiled broadly. She truly felt justified and fair now, envisioning the team the way it used to be, only wearing bras. It wasn't such a big price to pay, really. "We can all go shopping together tomorrow," she added.

Jeannie kicked at the pavement, her head bowed.

"Look, Nicky," Keescha said, "wear a bra if you want. I don't care. It's not going to make you a better ball player, and it's not going to get you the team captain position."

"The team is ruined," Jeannie said softly.

"No, it's not!" Keescha said.

Nicky cleared her throat. "The way things are going now, Keescha, the Daffodils are doomed. You saw how we played against the Clippers. Like I said, there's no going back. But my plan will get us back together."

"We just had a bad day yesterday," Keescha argued. "It was only our first game! Remember how good we were at that first practice?"

"That was before Caitlin got team captain!" Nicky said. "Now we aren't playing *together*, Keescha. We aren't a team. We've got to change together, or we're sunk."

Both Keescha and Jeannie looked at Nicky then, and there was a distinct feeling of doom. Nicky noticed three leftover tulip bulbs blooming in Mrs. Kline's third-grade classroom window. Every year, Mrs. Kline had her class force red tulip bulbs into bloom early, starting the project in November (they would normally bloom in late March), so they'd be ready for Valentine's Day gifts to the parents.

Nicky remembered Mrs. Kline's explanation. "I've kept the bulbs in the refrigerator, but now we'll plant them in our warm classroom, boys and girls. They'll think it's spring and bloom!"

The picture of the team as a field of spring flowers dazzled Nicky. She truly was the team captain, whistle or no whistle. "The Daffodils," she said quietly to herself, "are really going to bloom this year."

"What did you say?" Jeannie asked Nicky.

"Nothing. Jeannie, do you want to get a bra?"

Jeannie shrugged, then said, "Let's play hop-scotch before the bell rings."

Picking up a rock, Nicky said, "Okay. This is my marker. Let's play."

◇ 9 ◇

Hurt on the Inside

"Did you talk to Claire?" Nicky asked her father breathlessly the second she walked through the door. Emily straggled behind on the driveway. "Can she take me to Lamonts today, or tomorrow?"

"Next week she can," Mr. Durbin said in a pleased voice. "How's that?" He stood at the kitchen counter drinking orange juice and watching Emily chase a butterfly. The high school got out earlier than the elementary school, so he was home when Nicky and Emily arrived.

Nicky groaned.

"Are you bouncing *that* much?" Mr. Durbin asked.

Disappointment threatened to swallow Nicky up. She wanted the bra for the Daffodil practice on Saturday afternoon.

"You know, Dad, I was thinking," Nicky said, choosing her words carefully so she wouldn't seem ungrateful. "I can try on bras *myself*. It's really not that big a deal. You could drop me off at the mall and pick me up later, you know? Maybe even a couple of my friends could come, too."

Mr. Durbin frowned. "I'm not going to just drop you off at the mall," he said.

"Why not?" Nicky said, making a heroic effort to keep the whine out of her voice.

"Because."

"Because why?"

"Nicky."

"I mean it, Dad. I'd only be there for half an hour. You could go to Ernst Hardware." Nicky knew how her father loved hardware stores.

"Half an hour?" Mr. Durbin said. He stared at the kitchen counter.

"Dad?"

"Half an hour, okay, okay. I'll be in the men's department, though. I'm not leaving the store."

"And can a couple of my friends come, too? For moral support?"

"Okay," he said.

"Thank you, Dad!" Nicky ran over and hugged her father, burying her face in his corduroy sport coat. Mr. Durbin set his glass on the counter and hugged his daughter back.

Emily came in the front door a few minutes later. Nicky was dipping graham crackers into a tall glass of chocolate milk, and Mr. Durbin was upstairs changing his clothes.

"Hi, Nicky!" Emily cried and tossed her pink lunch box onto the kitchen counter.

"You don't have to yell, Em," Nicky said. What color should she get? A dark color would show through her white shirts. She wanted everyone to know she had a bra, but she didn't want to show the world every detail like Caitlin did.

"Nicky, are you getting a bra today, or can you play?"

"I'm going to Lamonts tomorrow morning," Nicky said. She noticed that Emily seemed not to care one way or another about bras, whether they existed or not. She just wanted to play. Nicky vaguely remembered the feeling of not caring, too. That seemed a thousand years ago.

"Then can you watch me do a front hip circle?"

"I guess," Nicky said. "Let me finish this first."

"I'll meet you in the backyard!" Emily shouted and ran for the door.

She was practicing the hip circles when Nicky finally came out. "Watch, Nicky!" Emily stopped in the middle of a circle, hanging sideways on the bar, then scrambled to the gymnast's starting position. Glancing at Nicky, but not moving her head, Emily stretched her body tall and wiped the smile off her face with the back of her hand. She looked at her sister one last time to make sure she was really watching.

"I'm watching, I'm watching," Nicky said and crossed her arms over her chest. "Go on, already!"

Emily waited a second or two more, then placed her hands on the bar. She pulled herself up, still not smiling, then with her hipbones stuck to the bar as if they'd been super-glued there, she dropped her head forward and around the bar and came back up looking through long strings of brown hair, but without cracking her serious expression.

Nicky clapped. "That's terrific, Em!" she sang out.

Only after Emily dropped off the bar did she allow herself a triumphant grin. "I told you I could do it," she said.

"Doesn't it feel good to whip around like

that?" Nicky asked, getting excited herself.

Emily nodded. "Yeah," she said.

"Let me do it now." Nicky moved into position in front of the bar. She pulled herself up, then threw her head forward. Around the bar she went once, then at the top she dropped over again, and around a second time, then a third, then a fourth. Each turn got faster with less hesitation at the top. Finally, after the fifth turn, she pushed off away from the bar and tossed her head back and her chest forward, in the finishing stance.

"Wow," Emily said, her eyes bright with admiration.

"It's easy," Nicky said. She brushed her hands together.

Emily pouted slightly. "I can't do that."

"You'll learn it eventually," Nicky assured her. "Just keep practicing. I couldn't do it when I was your age, either."

Emily nodded.

Nicky walked around to the swings. She sat on the left one, her favorite, and started to pump. She swung higher and higher until she was just even with the neighbor's fence, then she let go, punched out her arms and legs so her body made a perfect "X," shouted "Hey!", then dropped.

She'd spent too much time in the glorious "X,"

though. She couldn't straighten her legs, and she fell hard on her bottom.

Emily's eyes practically popped out of her head. She burst into laughter. Anger sizzled up Nicky's spine, along with the pain from falling.

Emily looked at her big sister's grim expression and quit laughing.

"See if I ever do gymnastics with you again!" Nicky shouted, jumping up and slapping the dirt from her jeans. She stomped back into the house.

Fifteen minutes later, after Nicky had cried herself out, there was a soft knocking on her door. "Nicky?" said a little voice.

"Go away," Nicky said. Her anger had diluted like watercolors in her tears, and all that was left were hurt feelings. She who had fallen off the bars tons of times, and who had also giggled when her friends had fallen, *she* now actually wanted to die because little Emily had laughed. She was surprised at herself.

She glanced at the framed picture of last year's Daffodils beside her bed. Two rows of yellow Daffodils with caps, bats, and mitts. No tie-dyed shirts, no bras, no lipstick. Nicky stood next to the coach, at the far end of the first row, touching the whistle that hung from her neck. The feeling she had now when she looked at that whistle matched the hurt from falling in front of Emily, and hearing Emily's laughter.

Caitlin always seemed to be laughing.

"Nicky, I didn't mean to laugh at you," the voice said again.

Nicky said nothing.

"Can I come in?"

"If you want," Nicky said grudgingly.

The door creaked open. Emily's eyes shone with tears of her own. "I'm sorry," she said.

Nicky gave Emily a serious look. "It's all right, I guess."

Emily sucked in a breath so hard, she shuddered.

"Just don't do it again. You've got to learn about people's feelings." Suddenly she remembered something her kindergarten teacher used to say. "You can hurt someone just as badly on the inside as on the outside," she quoted to Emily.

Emily was too upset to do anything but nod. Fresh tears pooled in her eyes.

Nicky couldn't help but smile. Little kids' eyes could hold more tears than older people's could, she thought.

"Would you hit some balls with me?" Nicky asked softly.

Emily wiped her eyes. "Okay," she said.

◇ 10 ◇
These Are Friends?

Later that evening, Nicky sat down at her father's desk and dialed Jeannie's number. "Hello, Fritz, is Jeannie there?" Nicky said.

"Yeah. Hold on." It sounded as if he dropped the receiver on the floor from the bang that echoed in Nicky's ear. She knew that Fritz had probably set the phone on a TV tray. Jeannie's mom worked swing shift at Fred Meyer. Fritz and Jeannie ate lots of TV dinners.

"Hi, it's me," Nicky said when Jeannie lifted the receiver.

"Hi, me," Jeannie said.

"Jeannie, my dad's going to take me to the mall tomorrow morning to get a bra. Do you want to come?"

"I don't know."

"You can get a bra, too!" Nicky said.

Jeannie was quiet. Then, finally, she said, "I don't want one."

"Why not?" Nicky said.

"I just don't," Jeannie said. "They look uncomfortable."

Nicky was quiet. Why hadn't Jeannie said that at school? Nicky remembered asking her directly. "I'm still going to get one," Nicky said.

"I'll go with you," Jeannie offered.

"Really?"

"Yeah."

"Thanks. We'll pick you up at nine, then, okay?"

"Okay."

Nicky waited for Jeannie to say something else, but she didn't. "Bye, Jeannie," Nicky said.

"Bye."

Nicky thought about Jeannie. It *would* look kind of ridiculous, she had to admit, for Jeannie to wear a bra. Jeannie was the smallest kid in the class. She hadn't had a pimple yet. Several of the girls, including Nicky, had had their first pimple already. But Jeannie could have been more enthusiastic, Nicky thought, for my sake.

With a sigh, Nicky dialed Keescha's number. This call would be even tougher, Nicky thought, but Keescha had to understand why Nicky was doing this. It was for the team.

When the phone rang, Mr. Conn's answering machine came on. *"Hello, you have reached the home of Alex Conn —* Hello?" The message was interrupted by a real human voice. It was Keescha's father.

"Is Keescha there?" Nicky said.

"One moment, please."

Nicky heard footsteps across what sounded like a kitchen floor, and then muffled arguing. All Nicky could make out was Mr. Conn saying, *"Ten minutes."*

"Yeah?" Keescha said when she picked up the receiver.

"This is Nicky."

"Hey, Nicky, what's up?"

"I know how you feel about bras, but I was wondering if you wanted to go to Lamonts with me and Jeannie tomorrow morning before practice. Help *me* pick out a bra."

Keescha was silent, just as Jeannie had been. Nicky grew more irritated. "Keescha?" she said.

"You're really stuck on this idea, aren't you?"

"Yes. Do you want to come or not?"

"I'll come, I'll come. But just to keep you from getting something really ugly."

"Thanks a lot," Nicky said sarcastically.

"At your service."

"Nine o'clock, then."

"Right," Keescha said.

"Okay. See you tomorrow morning."

Nicky sat hunched over the phone at her father's desk. Neither Jeannie nor Keescha had been very supportive. She shouldn't be surprised, she told herself, but on the other hand, *they were her friends*. You'd think they could at least be encouraging, wish her luck because she was at least *trying* to attract the other girls and keep the team together, or offer another idea. But, *no*. It was all up to her.

Nicky stood up, slammed the chair into the desk, then stomped down the hall to her room.

◇ 11 ◇
The Bra Safari

Keescha squeezed into the back of the Durbins' Toyota with Jeannie and Nicky. Emily sat in the front, wearing her lavender gymnastics outfit, ready to be dropped off at Gymboree.

Nicky had cooled down from the night before. She hadn't expected this, but now she felt uncomfortable with the whole idea of getting a bra. What was she doing anyway, buying a *bra*?

"Are you going to get a bra, too, Keescha?" Emily asked suddenly.

"Are you kidding?" Keescha said. "No way."

"Nicky says she bounces, that's why she needs one."

Nicky covered her face with both hands.

Keescha grinned. "I like to bounce," she said. Emily giggled.

Mercifully, Mr. Durbin began asking Emily questions about gymnastics, and Emily took the bait.

"Has your sister ever *seen* a bra?" Keescha whispered to Nicky, as if her sister were an alien who had just arrived on planet Earth.

"Of course, she has," Nicky said in her most mature voice.

Humiliation engulfed Nicky. She was sorry she'd invited Keescha and Jeannie to go with her, she was sorry her father was driving them, she was sorry she was even a girl. She could hardly believe that getting a bra could make such a difference in her life.

Mr. Durbin took Emily into her class at Gymboree at one end of the mall, then drove across the parking lot to Lamonts. "Here we are," he said, trying to smile at Nicky, Keescha, and Jeannie. "Happy hunting," he added.

"Dad!" Nicky cried.

Keescha laughed. "We're going on a bra safari." She raised an imaginary rifle to her eye.

"Yeah," Jeannie said, giggling, "it's a jungle out there."

"Wanted: One bra, dead or alive!" Keescha

said and howled, falling back against the seat.

"I'm sorry, Nicky," her father said. "I hope you find a bra you like."

"Thanks," she said hastily. She had never wanted anything so badly as to get out of that car.

She rushed ahead of Jeannie and Keescha into the store, and then into the lingerie department. An entire rack of little boxes labeled "Preteens" caught her eye. Pictures of girls smiled out at her from the boxes. How could they be smiling like that? Nicky thought. They were wearing nothing from the waist up but skimpy little bras.

Nicky opened one of the boxes and pulled out a pale yellow bra made of T-shirt material with a little lace around the edges. It looked okay.

"Isn't this pretty?" she said to Jeannie.

"Hey, look!" Keescha called from the next rack down.

Nicky glanced over to see her friend holding a huge, monster bra across her chest.

"Do you think it's my size?" Keescha asked, smiling.

Nicky stared at Keescha and frowned. Jeannie turned red with embarrassment.

"Do you think it will keep me from *bouncing*?" Keescha held the bra at arm's length and examined it. "It might keep my *head* from bouncing, nothing else," she said, pulling the immense cup down over her black curls.

Nicky scowled. She saw the young saleswoman coming, smiling warmly and picking her way between the racks. Nicky signaled for Keescha to cut it out.

Jeannie was laughing, bubbling over with giggles. She was as bad as Emily, practically.

Nicky felt relieved when the saleswoman arrived. She wore a silky pink dress and high heels. She knows what she's doing, Nicky thought.

"I'd like to buy a bra," Nicky said.

"Oh, wonderful!" the woman gushed. "There are so many cute bras for girls today."

Keescha guffawed.

"And I see you've already found your choices!" the saleswoman said, ignoring Keescha. Her voice seemed to boom throughout the entire store. "Did you see any other styles you like?"

"I don't know my cup size," Nicky said quietly.

The saleswoman laughed. "With these bras, honey, there's no cup size. It's *one-size-fits-all*."

"You only need cups if you're big like me," Keescha said, patting her chest.

"Yes, well." The saleswoman cleared her

throat and stretched her lips into a pained smile.

Jeannie edged around the side of the rack and giggled.

Nicky felt bewildered and embarrassed. It wasn't funny. Keescha and Jeannie weren't helping at all. She frowned at them. She wanted them to be quiet and act mature.

"How about this one, too?" the saleswoman said, glancing at the box Nicky clutched under her arm. She pulled a box from the rack. "This is our most popular style."

"Okay," Nicky said.

"You can try them on back here, honey."

Nicky marched ahead of Keescha and Jeannie to the dressing room. When all three of them were squished into one of the cubicles, Nicky opened the boxes. She didn't want to show her bare chest to her friends, so she turned around and pulled off her Daffodil T-shirt.

"I want to try one on, too," Keescha said in a prissy voice.

"Don't," Nicky said, her back still turned.

"Why not?"

Nicky hesitated. Keescha was making fun of her. "It's not your size, you said so yourself."

Keescha didn't answer Nicky. "Hey, Jeannie," Keescha said, "do you know how you can tell if you're ready for a bra?"

"How?" Jeannie said softly.

As Nicky hooked the front of the bra together against her chestbone, she could hear Keescha behind her, sorting through her purse. When she turned around, Keescha offered her two pencils. "Wedge these under your breasts, Nicky. If they don't drop, you're ready."

Jeannie covered her mouth to muffle her snorts of laughter.

Nicky had thought that she hated Caitlin the day they lost to the Clippers when Caitlin didn't seem to care, but she was wrong. What she felt for Keescha and Jeannie now was deeper. *This* was hate. They were supposed to be her friends, and here they were, acting like idiots!

"Knock it off, Keescha!" Nicky said.

"Have you found something yet, dear?" the saleswoman called from outside the beige curtain.

"Yes," Nicky said, turning around quickly in case the saleswoman barged in.

"Wonderful! I'll be right outside here to ring you up when you're finished."

"Thank you," Nicky said.

"She's going to ring you up!" Keescha said.

Jeannie's eyes widened as she got Keescha's dumb joke. "You won't be home, though," Jeannie said. "She'll have to call back later."

Every movement, every word, made Nicky angrier. She tore the bra off, yanked on her T-shirt, and stomped out of the dressing room.

"Nicky's mad," she heard Jeannie say through the curtain.

"So?" said Keescha. "It's her own fault."

"They made fun of me," Nicky said to her father. It was later in the afternoon, and they were alone in the car, on the way to Daffodil practice.

"I'm sorry, sweetheart. I guess I didn't help any by joking in the parking lot."

Nicky shrugged. It wasn't her father's fault, really. "It's not that, Dad," she said. She yanked at her new bra, which was inching up and driving her crazy. Also, for some reason, the bra was making her sweat heavily. Drops of perspiration soaked the elastic and itched. "Jeannie and Keescha don't care about what's happening to the team. Keescha thinks I just want to be team captain, but that's not true."

"Hmm."

"Of course I wish I were captain," Nicky explained quickly. "It's just that — well, I don't know. Things are weird right now."

"Because of this new girl? What's her name again?"

"*Caitlin*." Nicky practically spat the name out. "I don't know who I hate more — Caitlin, or Keescha and Jeannie."

"Are you sure you want to go to practice?" her father asked, taking his eyes off the road for a moment.

"I *have* to, Dad," Nicky said. "I can't just not show up." She was surprised at her father. He was the one who always harped about commitment and responsibility.

"I suppose so," Dad said.

Nicky stared ahead and straightened her Daffodil cap. She was catcher, and that's all she would think about this afternoon. Catching balls. Giving good pitching signals to Keescha (the serious ones), throwing accurately to the rest of the team in the infield. Think about that, she told herself.

When they arrived in the parking area, Nicky could see that Caitlin and Coach Kwock were leading the team in warm-up stretches. She saw Keescha in the front row, but she couldn't spot Jeannie.

"See ya later," Nicky said to her father as she scrambled out of the car. She felt better already, just seeing the Daffodils out there together.

◇ 12 ◇
Walls of Dolls

Nicky darted across the field to the team. Her bra felt like a bug crawling under her shirt, and she grabbed at it as she ran. She wished she could glue it in place. Nicky wanted Jan and the other Daffodils to think she got the bra because of necessity and maturation; it wouldn't do to claw at it miserably all during practice.

No one called out to greet her when she arrived. The coach had just sent half the team out to run around the field while she and Caitlin started hitting balls to the rest of the team. Nicky had to admit that Caitlin could really play ball when she wanted to.

Nicky waited by the bench for a second, but still no one said, "Hey, Nicky's here!" or "Hi,

Nicky!" At least Caitlin isn't getting all the attention, either, she told herself. Everyone is working hard, the way they are supposed to. She did a couple of stretches.

She was strapping on her shinguards when she heard a quiet voice nearby. "Hi, Nicky." It was Jeannie.

"Hi."

There was no sign of laughter in Jeannie's face now. In fact, Jeannie looked as if some air had been let out of her since the morning. Her shoulders sagged, and her Daffodil cap seemed even bigger than usual.

Nicky felt the last remnant of her anger melt away. "Ready for practice?" she asked.

"I guess."

"Get a couple of balls, then, and throw me some grounders." Nicky reached for her catcher's mask. It lay on the bench with the other equipment. Had Caitlin done this?

"Hey, Nicky," came a familiar voice. Nicky looked up. It was Jan. She had finished her lap around the field. "Did you get a bra?" she said. Jan was looking at the indentation along Nicky's back. She wore orange lipstick — surely from Caitlin's vast collection — and a broad, friendly smile.

"Yeah, I did," Nicky said and smiled back.

She looked again and noticed another change. "I like your hair," Nicky said, honestly admiring Jan's French braid. "Is your cap going to ruin it?"

Jan shook her head. She carefully clamped on her yellow cap and adjusted the braid. Her fingernail polish was green.

Nicky stood straight and gave an A-okay sign to Jan.

"You want me to do your hair, too?" Jan asked Nicky. "I did Erin's and Susan's."

Erin and Susan had arrived at the bench, panting, while Jan was talking. They turned when they heard their names, smiled coyly, patted their braids gently like models, then dissolved into giggles.

Nicky smiled and glanced at Jeannie, who had pulled her cap lower over her eyes. Then she scanned the area for Keescha. She was behind the backstop with Coach Kwock. "Is my hair long enough?" Nicky asked.

"Sure! It'd look really neat, too, Nicky. Your hair's so thick."

Erin said, "Oooo, yeah, Nicky!"

Jan was still her friend after all, Nicky thought. She could tell. "Okay," said Nicky. "Why not?"

"Sit here," Jan said.

"Right now?" Nicky could see Jeannie back away out of the corner of her eye.

"I can do it really fast," said Jan. "Caitlin taught me."

Nicky took her cap off, and Jan started to brush her dark hair. "Your hair has got natural highlights, Nicky," Jan said as she began to separate the hair on the top of Nicky's head into three sections.

Suddenly Erin said to Susan, "Did Caitlin show you this note, yet?"

"No," Susan said, squinting. She still wasn't wearing her glasses.

"It's *great*," Erin said, handing the note to Susan. "It's to *Greg*!"

Susan pushed the note away. "I can't read it," she said. "I don't have my glasses."

"Did you lose them?" Nicky asked. Jan was halfway down the back of Nicky's head now. Her fingers were strong, and she pulled the hair tightly, but it didn't hurt.

"No. I'm getting contacts for my birthday."

Nicky was surprised. "That's not until summer!" she said.

Susan mumbled something that Nicky didn't hear.

"Let *me* see the note, then," Jan said from behind Nicky.

Erin handed the paper to Nicky. "Here, Nicky, hold it up so Jan can read it. I've got to go to the bathroom before the infield drill starts." Nicky watched Erin race to the school building, then held the paper up for Jan to read. Caitlin had used pink ink, and her handwriting was round and loopy. Jan read out loud.

" *'Dear Greg. Do you want to go to the next Hardboiled Egg concert with me? My brother works for them, the Eggs, I mean, and he can get us in. It's next Friday nite. Tell me at recess, okay? Love, Caitlin.'* Oooo!" Jan's eyes grew wide. "She signed it *love!*" Jan added.

Nicky glanced at Jeannie. She sat at the end of the bench and made circles in the dirt with the toe of her shoe.

"Susan, do you have a rubber band?" Jan said. "I'm finished with Nicky's braid."

"I've got one," Caitlin said, jogging up to the group. She pulled a purple rubber band out of her jeans pocket and handed it to Jan. "Your hair looks really cute," she said to Nicky.

Nicky searched Caitlin's face for a snide smile or a hint of meanness, but it wasn't there. Caitlin seemed totally enchanted with Nicky's cuteness. As Nicky puzzled over this, she noticed Keescha and Coach Kwock and the rest of the team walking toward the bench. Nicky stood up.

Maybe the sight of Keescha gave Jeannie confidence, or maybe the fact that more of the team was around now so Caitlin's group wasn't such a big deal to Jeannie — whatever the reason, Jeannie suddenly stood up, too, and shuffled over to stand next to Nicky. "Nicky?" she said.

"Yeah."

"Nicky, I was wondering. After practice, do you want to come over and play dolls?"

Nicky stiffened. Here she was actually bridging the gap, bringing the team together, and then Jeannie drops this bomb. *"No,"* Nicky said. "NO."

Keescha's eyebrows popped up.

"No offense, Jeannie," Erin said, looking at Jeannie with disdain, "but you are *such* a baby."

Caitlin pulled the captain's whistle back and forth on its chain. "It's okay for her to be immature," she said to Erin. She looked at Jeannie then. "After all, she's only *ten.*"

Jeannie sank two inches shorter. "So? At least I act my age, not my *shoe size*," she said, her cheeks crayon red beneath her gigantic cap.

Caitlin hooted with laughter. Erin and Jan joined in. "I see what you mean!" Erin said.

Jeannie looked up at Nicky just as Emily often did when she was hurt.

Nicky pulled against her own strong impulse

to rescue Jeannie. She cared about Jeannie, but keeping the team together was more important. And not only that, Nicky decided in that instant, Jeannie *was* acting like a baby.

Keescha stomped over to the bench. "Get off Jeannie's case," she said to Caitlin.

Nicky couldn't believe Keescha was backing Jeannie like this. It felt as if Keescha were saying to Nicky, "If you're going to abandon her, then *I'll* take care of her!"

"I wasn't talking to you," Caitlin said evenly.

"Well *I'm* talking to *you*," said Keescha. "Jeannie's little, but she's fast."

"Not fast enough," Jan said and elbowed Erin, who stood next to her. They laughed again.

"Don't slam her," Keescha said.

Caitlin gazed coolly at Keescha, raised the silver whistle to her strawberry pink lips, and blew. There was no reason for her to blow it then, Nicky thought, except to show Keescha who was boss. "Time for practice," she said.

"Some team captain," Keescha scoffed.

"Girls?" Coach Kwock called from the other bench. "Get out there! Come on!"

"Let's see you hit one to Seattle, Jan," Caitlin said, and she walked away with Jan, Erin, and Susan at her heels.

"Twit," Keescha said to Nicky and Jeannie.

She smacked the ball she was holding into her mitt.

Nicky didn't respond.

Jeannie ducked her head, peeking at Nicky from the corner of her eye.

"You were right about her screwing us up, Nicky," Keescha said. "She plays good enough, but *she is a twit*."

Nicky looked at Keescha and thought, you don't have to call names, but she said, "Let's go play."

◇13◇
Taking Notes

"What am I going to do?" Jeannie asked Nicky Monday morning on the bus.

"About what?" Nicky asked.

Jeannie pouted. *"Niiickyyy."*

"What?"

"About Caitlin teasing me," Jeannie whined.

Nicky looked out the window as the bus passed the remnant of a tree house. Strips of board hung in the bare branches of an alder tree by the side of the road. She turned to look at Jeannie. "Couldn't you tell that Caitlin isn't into dolls?"

Jeannie sat back against her seat.

"I'm sorry, Jeannie, but I don't see what I can do."

"Who said I was asking you to do anything?" Jeannie said.

"I thought you did."

"I *didn't*."

"Fine." Nicky looked out the window again.

When they got to school, Jeannie pushed off the bus ahead of Nicky and ran to the classroom. Nicky didn't care.

Later, during Social Studies time, the class was supposed to be writing answers to questions about India's imports and exports. There were ten minutes left until recess, and Nicky sat at her desk and watched Caitlin and Erin passing notes.

Jeannie was playing with toy ponies in her desk, and Keescha's eyes were closed.

Caitlin had her book propped up on her desk as a shield to Mrs. Sirmyer. Nicky watched as she passed a note to Erin. Erin read it, scribbled her own note, and then passed it back to Caitlin. Nicky was shocked when Erin looked up and signaled to her. "A note for you," she mouthed.

"Me?" Nicky mouthed back.

Erin nodded. So did Caitlin.

What could they want? Nicky wondered. They had certainly been nice to her Saturday at practice. Suddenly she had an incredible thought: Maybe Erin and Jan had told Caitlin what a terrific captain Nicky had been last year. Maybe they wanted her to be *co*-captain of the team! Could it be?

Nicky's best excuse to travel across the room and get Caitlin's note was a trip to the waste basket. Caitlin's desk was on the way. Unfortunately, Jeffrey Barnett sat right by the waste basket. He put mousse in his red hair, wore the same green shirt every day, and he smelled like fried chicken. Nicky hoped he wouldn't bug her when she passed; he was always trying to get involved in her business. But she had to get that note from Caitlin.

Nicky ripped a sheet of paper from her Social Studies notebook, stood up, and walked purposefully to the waste basket. Jeffrey turned to watch her. Caitlin had the note ready to pass to Nicky on her way back to her seat.

Just as Nicky dropped the wad of paper in the trash, she heard a scuffle and a little shriek. It was a Caitlin shriek.

Mrs. Sirmyer looked up from her pile of papers. "What's going on there?"

"Jeffrey took something of mine," Caitlin said.

"Caitlin was passing notes," Jeffrey shot back. "I couldn't concentrate on my work."

Several members of the class laughed. Kee-scha hooted.

"Do you have Caitlin's note?" Mrs. Sirmyer asked Jeffrey.

"Yes, he does!" Caitlin cried. "It's my property. I want it back."

"You have a choice, then," Mrs. Sirmyer said, leaning forward on her elbows. "Jeffrey can hand your property in to me, since you are not to be passing notes in class, and I'm not sure what I'll do with it, or he can throw it in the garbage."

Caitlin glared at Mrs. Sirmyer. "That's not fair. It's *mine*."

"What's not fair, Miss Whiteside, is the disruption your note passing is causing this classroom." She looked away from Caitlin, somehow taking in every single eye in the room. Nicky stood en route to the waste basket. It was as if everyone in the classroom had been frozen in place.

Mrs. Sirmyer focused back on Caitlin. "What's it going to be?"

Wisely, Nicky thought, Caitlin said, "Trash."

Jeffrey nodded to Mrs. Sirmyer and then grinned at Nicky.

Now only Jeffrey was thawed. He stood, marched to the waste basket and, with two fin-

gers, dropped the small wad as if it were a soiled
Kleenex. He marched back and plopped into his
seat, and only then did the class breathe again.
Satisfied, Mrs. Sirmyer turned back to her
papers.

Nicky turned to head back to her desk. She
took a single step, then her eye caught a flash
of movement from Jeffrey's desk. He still had
Caitlin's note! It was open, and he motioned,
very discreetly, to Nicky.

"Want it?" he whispered.

Nicky nodded.

"What you gonna give me for it?"

Nicky looked up to see if anyone was watching. Scotty Clatworthy was, of course. He sat
next to Jeffrey. Jeannie and Keescha were the
only other interested parties. Caitlin and Erin
appeared to be writing more notes.

"Money?" Nicky offered, very softly.

Jeffrey shook his head and grinned. He elbowed Scotty in the ribs.

Nicky bristled. Anger rushed through her
body, but her expression remained calm. At all
costs, Nicky would keep her reaction to a bare
minimum. *"What, then?"* she said, a little
louder.

His cheeks grew pink, then he puckered his
lips and made a vulgar kissing motion.

Mrs. Sirmyer looked up.

"Slimeball," Nicky said and trounced back to her desk. What did she need that note for, anyway? She could just ask Erin what it had said at recess.

When the bell rang two minutes later, Nicky walked straight to Erin's desk. "What did you want?" Nicky asked.

Erin looked at Caitlin. "It's about recess, Nicky."

"What about it?"

"Uh," Erin began, her eyes shifting back and forth from Nicky to Caitlin. "We really like you, Nicky," she said.

Nicky smiled. She just knew what Erin was going to say! She could hear it already. . . . *And we want you to be team captain again.* . . .

"The thing is," Caitlin said loudly, "we like *you*, Nicky, but if you hang around with Keescha and Jeannie at recess, you can't be with us."

Nicky blinked, then laughed nervously. "I can't?" she said.

"No."

"How about if I play with them this recess, and with you guys after lunch?"

"Come on, Erin," Caitlin said. "Let's go *play*." She said it sarcastically, just like she had the week before.

Erin followed Caitlin out the door, leaving Nicky alone, or almost alone. She clenched her fists and would have sworn if Jeffrey hadn't suddenly emerged from the coat closet. "Hi, Nicky," he said.

"I know what the note said," Nicky snapped. "But I just fou — "

"Taking that note was *so* immature," she said. "Don't do it again."

"Nicky, I found *another* note. It's not about recess, either. It's about you." Some melted mousse beaded on Jeffrey's forehead.

"It's a stupid note," Scotty said, but he was blushing. "Come on, Jeffrey, let's go."

"So what if it's about me! So what if I *do* want the note?" Nicky said. "No way am I, you know, kissing you just to read it."

Jeffrey blushed deeply and then he grinned. Nicky realized that he might have given her the note a second ago, but not anymore. "Give me the note!" she demanded.

He grinned again.

"Look, how about a phone call?" Nicky said.

"Huh?"

"You can call me, and I'll talk to you on the telephone," she explained, then added, "for fifteen minutes."

Jeffrey considered this. "I don't know — "

"Twenty," Nicky said.

"*You* call *me*, and you've got a deal."

"Okay. Hand it over."

"Nooo waaaaay. You have to deliver the goods first, Cutes." He checked this remark out with Scotty with another jab to Scotty's ribs. Scotty blushed.

Nicky breathed deeply, for control. I could crush this wimp if I wanted to, she told herself. "I'll call you tonight."

"I'll give you the note tomorrow, then."

"Fine," Nicky said. She ripped a corner off her Social Studies homework assignment. "Write down your phone number."

"Oh, okay. If you insist." He smiled at her again — he looked like a grinning chimpanzee, Nicky thought — and scrawled his number with her pencil.

When he and Scotty left, Nicky was alone in the classroom. She looked at the clock. Ten minutes left in recess. Who would she play with if she went out, Keescha and Jeannie, or Erin and Jan? She didn't know.

She decided to stay in this recess, as if she were in trouble. Funny, she thought. She'd take the Mrs. Sirmyer kind of trouble any day over this.

◇ 14 ◇
A Fish Sticks
Kind of Evening

Nicky sat at the dinner table, slumped in her chair, staring in disgust at her fish sticks and string beans. Her emotions were so strong that she was surprised her father didn't ask her what was wrong.

She decided, as she stared at those fish sticks, that she felt like a fisherman who had a huge catch in his net. Five million wiggling, slimy fish, not cooperating with him.

"Do you know what I wish I had?" Mr. Durbin suddenly asked his daughters.

"A motorcycle," Emily said.

Nicky groaned. Emily would turn any question a person asked into a guessing game.

"No," said Mr. Durbin, "it has to do with this house. Try again."

"A new chair!"

"No."

"A movie to watch tonight!"

"No, that's not it, either."

Emily scowled. "I give up," she said.

"Do you give up, too, Nicky?" Mr. Durbin asked.

"I'm not even playing," Nicky said sourly. She didn't like the idea of her father wanting something.

"Okay. I wish I had an infrared map of this house, where the dirtiest places would show up as red, and the rest either clean white or only slightly pink." He moved his hands in the air beside him, taking in the entire kitchen. "Then I could just look at it and say, 'Oh, the kitchen floor is red, I'll do that this weekend.' "

Both Emily and Nicky just stared at their father.

"Wouldn't that be terrific, gang?" he asked them.

"How was I supposed to guess *that*!" Emily cried in disgust.

Mr. Durbin smiled. "I didn't expect you to try to guess, honey." He reached over and brushed his hand across Emily's sandy brown hair.

"*Dad*," Nicky said. "*I* clean the bathroom and vacuum and dust!" It seemed as if she had to do everything! Clean the house, console her tired father, teach Emily about bras, choose between her friends!

"I know you do, Nicky," Mr. Durbin said, "and I appreciate it. You don't have to jump all over me, though, do you?"

"I'm *not*!" Nicky said. "I'm just telling you what *I* do!"

Mr. Durbin's glasses slipped down his nose. "I know that." He pushed his glasses back. "I don't know what I'd do without your help."

Tears pooled in Nicky's eyes. "Excuse me!" she said, pushing her chair back from the table and running out of the kitchen.

She paused around the corner and heard her father say, in a confused and helpless voice, "Looks like Nicky's becoming a teenager, doesn't it?"

Nicky bounded up the stairs and slammed her bedroom door.

She sulked in her room awhile, then remembered the grueling call she had to make that evening. Jeffrey "Slimeball" Barnett. Like it or not, she did want to know what was in the note he'd found about her. Grudgingly, she went into her father's room and dialed the number Jeffrey had scrawled on the scrap of paper.

"Hello, is Jeffrey there?"

"It's me," Jeffrey said.

"This is Nicky."

"Hi, Nicky." His voice was so soft, she hardly recognized it.

"So, I'm calling. What did you want to talk about?" She wasn't going to make this easy for him.

"Uh, I don't know."

"Why can't you just tell me what's in the note?" Nicky asked.

"Well, uh, it's kinda personal."

"Who wrote it?"

"I don't know," Jeffrey said. "It's not signed."

"Oh." Nicky squeezed the phone hard, the way she had held the bat last year before she belted her grand slam. The team had named it the luckiest bat.

"To tell you the truth, it's not very nice," Jeffrey said.

"Oh," Nicky said again.

They were silent.

"So what do you want to talk about?" Nicky repeated.

"I don't know."

"Do you want to talk about school?"

"Uh, not really."

Silence again.

"You know my softball team has its second game on Wednesday?"

"Really?"

"Yeah. We're the Daffodils." She waited for him to say something obnoxious like Dorky-dills, but he didn't. She went on. "We were the champs last year."

"My dad took me to a Mariner game last year," Jeffrey said. "Ken Griffey, Jr., hit two homers."

"You know what, Jeffrey?"

"What?"

"This will sound weird, I know, so don't laugh. Okay?"

"I won't."

"I want to manage a professional baseball team when I grow up." Nicky waited for Jeffrey to laugh.

"Really?"

"Yeah. I want to be a professional manager. You know, like a team captain."

"Are you team captain of the Daffodils?"

"I was last year."

"You must have done a good job if your team won." Jeffrey said the compliment very softly. Nicky's ear suddenly felt as if it were burning.

"Thanks," she said, moving the receiver to the other ear, to let the complimented one cool down.

"You're not the captain this year?" Jeffrey asked.

"No," Nicky said very softly.

"What?" said Jeffrey.

"No," she said louder. "Do you play ball?"

"Me? Naw. Soccer's my game. I'm a striker."

"You must be good," Nicky said, making an effort to return his compliment honestly. "Strikers and wings score all the points."

"Yeah. I'm small and quick."

Nicky blushed at this self-disclosure. He had just come right out and admitted his squirrel-ishness, as if it were a virtue. To Nicky, Jeffrey's size, together with his mousse and occasional smell, had been his chief flaws. But if he was a great striker, maybe being small was okay.

"I've got to go now," Nicky said after another ten-second lull.

"Okay. Oh, I've got an orthodontist appointment tomorrow, so I won't be at school. I'll bring the note by your softball practice, if that's okay."

"Just don't make a big deal of handing it to me."

"I won't. Thanks for calling, Nicky."

What choice did I have? Nicky wanted to say. "Don't forget the note," she said and hung up.

◇ 15 ◇
A Practice Disaster

It was the last fifteen minutes of practice. Nicky and Keescha were choosing bats for the practice game when Nicky saw Jeffrey and Scotty walking up to the fence.

"Caitlin," Coach Kwock said, pointing to the outfield, "run out and help collect the balls. It's time to play."

"Okay," Caitlin said. She blew the whistle and took off.

"Hi," Jeffrey called to Nicky.

Nicky put her hands on her hips, but she was also grinning. "What are you doing here?" she asked, even though she knew he was delivering the goods. Erin and Susan jogged up to Nicky and were listening.

"We're just here to watch," Jeffrey said, and slyly showed Nicky the edge of the note, sticking out of his pocket. "Isn't that right, Scotty?"

"Yeah," Scotty said, his face turning red. He carried his saxophone case. "If that's okay," he added, looking at Keescha. "Until my music lesson."

"I don't care," Keescha said.

"Me, neither," Nicky said. "Suit yourself." She decided to wait until Keescha wasn't around to get the note from Jeffrey.

Suddenly Caitlin came running in, squealing, "Boys!" She pointed to Jeffrey and Scotty.

"Geez," Keescha said. "You'd think they were the Lone Ranger and Tonto, cleverly disguised as Jeffrey Barnett and Scotty Clatworthy."

Jeannie stood next to Keescha, frowning.

All of the Daffodils were now crowded around Nicky at home plate. Erin, Jan, and Susan, who were all wearing makeup today, patted their crooked French braids and giggled.

"Boys," Coach Kwock called, "are you here for a reason?"

"We just want to watch," Jeffrey said.

"Do you mind if we have an audience today, girls?" the coach asked.

Everyone started talking and laughing.

Nicky really wanted Jeffrey to stay. She yelled for the team to shut up. "It's a free country," she said.

Caitlin scowled at Nicky. Nicky realized that she was taking over Caitlin's job, but she didn't care. Jeffrey was there because of her.

"I say we should vote," Caitlin said.

"Are we going to spend all practice on this?" Keescha said. *"Come on!"*

"Okay," Nicky said, "we can have a vote."

Jeffrey and Scotty still stood on the other side of the fence. They shifted from foot to foot and smiled painfully, as if they had unexpectedly been shoved on stage.

"All those who say it's okay for Jeffrey and Scotty to watch, raise your hands," Nicky said.

"I'm the team captain," Caitlin complained to Coach Kwock.

Nicky chafed at this, but Caitlin was right. She was the *official* captain, and Nicky didn't want any more trouble on the team. "Oh," Nicky said. "Yeah, well, I guess I forgot."

"Is this going to take all day?" Keescha said.

Coach Kwock cleared her throat. "This issue might come up again. We need to decide it. Go ahead, Caitlin."

"Raise your hand if the boys can watch," she declared to the team.

◇ 105

Nicky's hand shot up. The rest of the team followed, including Keescha, who raised her hand last and looked bored. Jeannie stood next to Keescha, her hand barely raised past her shoulder.

"You can stay," Caitlin said triumphantly to the boys.

"If you say one word, though," Keescha said to Jeffrey and Scotty, "I'm killing you both later."

Jeffrey saluted Keescha and looked very earnest. Nicky smiled.

"Twerp," Keescha said. She stalked to the pitcher's mound.

"Okay, team," Coach Kwock said, "let's go."

Nicky and the rest of the team jogged to their positions. Squatting behind the plate, Nicky pulled her face mask down.

Susan walked into the batter's box and tapped her bat on the plate. Then, ducking her head, she pulled her glasses out of her pocket and put them on.

Nicky gave the three-finger signal for Keescha to throw a sidespin. Susan swung hard, but late. Keescha grinned.

"Strike one!" Coach Kwock called. "Keep your eye on the ball, Susan. You swung too early."

Nicky threw the ball back to Keescha, then gave her the two-finger-then-one-finger signal for a backspin. Keescha wound up and threw.

Susan fouled the ball away. *"Damn,"* Susan said.

Nicky stared at Susan. She had never heard her friend swear before.

"Strike two," cried the coach. "Nice pitch, Keescha." She threw Keescha a new ball.

Nicky thought about the next pitch. It should be another sidespin, since Susan had gotten a piece of the backspin. Nicky shuffled behind the plate, then squatted again. When she held her glove up, her bra suddenly inched up under her armpits. She reached to yank at it, and Keescha frowned. Nicky had just given the signal to throw the ball to first base, that the runner was about to steal.

But there was no runner on first.

Keescha threw another curve, and Susan smacked it straight to third base. Jan missed it because she was looking at Jeffrey and Scotty.

"Pay attention!" Keescha cried.

"I am!" Jan shouted back.

Renee Kwock was next up to bat. Keescha glared at Nicky and fired a backspin across the plate before Nicky had a chance to give a signal.

Renee connected, popping the ball into center field. Erin missed it.

"Erin!" Keescha yelled.

"That's enough of that, Keescha," Coach Kwock called.

"A piece of mascara fell in my eye!" Erin cried. Even Nicky could see black stuff smudged on Erin's cheeks.

The coach called the team in.

"Let's talk for a minute," the coach said. "Sit on the bleachers."

When everyone was sitting, Coach Kwock began. "None of you seem to be concentrating."

"I wonder why?" Keescha said sarcastically and looked at Nicky.

Everyone watched Nicky and Keescha. No one said a word. Nicky wasn't sure what Keescha was getting at.

"You're a bunch of beauty queens!" Keescha said. "Everyone is so wrapped up in their bras, no pun intended."

The team laughed, then looked nervously around for Jeffrey and Scotty. They hadn't moved from the fence. There was no way they could hear.

"And that's *my* fault?" Nicky said, glaring first at Keescha, then over at Caitlin.

"Partly, yeah," Keescha said.

"*Girls*," Coach Kwock said in a warning voice.

"Miss Expert on Teams and Friends," Keescha said. "You only care about being team captain."

Nicky's eyes blinked rapidly five times, and she *never* blinked in an argument. "*You* don't care about the team," she said to Keescha. "I do!"

"Enough of this," Coach Kwock said. "I usually let these things settle on their own, but this is getting a little out of hand. I know today's practice was tough, but let's not say things we'll regret later."

Keescha folded her arms across her chest as if to say, "I'm not going to regret anything later."

Coach Kwock continued. "Tomorrow's our game against the Fenders. Let's all relax tonight, *think positively*, and we'll see you here tomorrow afternoon."

Everyone clapped once, the signal the practice was ended. Coach Kwock moved away with Taylor, Katie, and Renee to pack up the equipment.

Nicky was furious. Keescha had no right. There she stood on the pitcher's mound, yelling every time a Daffodil made a mistake, and then she had blamed Nicky!

Well, she'd show everyone, she thought. She

hadn't let Caitlin turn the team against her — Erin and Jan were still acting nice to her. She wouldn't let Keescha ruin things, either.

"See you, Jeannie," Keescha said. She took off her Daffodil cap and crumpled it into a ball.

Jeannie hadn't moved from her seat on the bleacher.

Just as Nicky was moving toward Keescha, to have a private conversation, she heard a scuffle and a shriek. "I got it!" Erin said. Jeffrey stood beside Erin, looking startled. Erin waved the note Jeffrey was going to give to Nicky high in the air.

"Oooo!" said Jan. "Read it!"

"That's not yours," Jeffrey protested. His face flushed angrily.

"What does it say?" Caitlin asked, rushing over.

"Give me a second," Erin said. She opened the paper as Caitlin, Jan, and Susan huddled around.

"Read it out loud," Susan said. "I can't see it."

Erin read. " *'Dear Jan,'* " she began.

"What was Jeffrey doing with a note to me?" Jan said.

Keescha, who stood on the outskirts of the group next to Nicky and Jeannie, glared at Jeffrey, but she listened along with everyone else.

Jeffrey looked at Nicky and shook his head. Then he covered his face with his hands.

"Who's it from?" Susan asked.

"It's not signed," answered Erin.

"Just read it," Caitlin said.

" *'I love Greg Gibbons sooo much,'* " Erin read. " *'He is so cute. Don't you think so? I couldn't believe it when he snapped my bra. Do you want to know a secret? Nicky Durbin doesn't need a bra. She should give it to her Barbie.'* "

Nicky gasped, and then stared at Caitlin.

"I didn't write that!" Caitlin said.

Keescha hooted. "How stupid," she said. "As if *anyone* here needs a bra."

"Yeah," Jeannie said, standing beside Keescha.

"How would *you* know?" Erin said to Jeannie.

"I didn't write that!" Caitlin cried again.

"Who did, then?" Nicky stepped closer to Erin to see the note. "It looks like your handwriting, Caitlin. And your pink ink!"

"Somebody must have stolen my pen!" Caitlin cried.

"*Sure.*" Nicky glared at Caitlin. "*Blame it on somebody else.* Just like it was your brother's idea to ruin the Daffodil shirts with tie-dye."

Caitlin looked at Erin and Jan, but this time,

◇ 111

they wouldn't look at *her*. She turned to Jeffrey. "Get out of here!" she said. "Get lost!"

"He wasn't going to show anyone the note," Nicky said in Jeffrey's defense. "He found it and was going to give it to me, secretly." Nicky glared at Caitlin. "It's not *his* fault, either."

"*I didn't do it,*" Caitlin said, glaring right back at Nicky.

Nicky turned and stalked away, across the field, by herself. Her fists were clenched, and her arms shook with fury.

◇16◇
Swinging Hard

Nicky slumped into the Toyota, slammed the door, then leaned her head against the window as Mr. Durbin pulled out of the lot. "Nicky?" he asked.

"Nicky?" Emily echoed from the backseat.

"I can't talk about it," Nicky said, choking on the words. Her rage was cooling away, leaving her with a sick, lukewarm humiliation. *Nicky Durbin doesn't need a bra. She should give it to her Barbie.* The words echoed in her head.

When they got home, it seemed as if Emily wanted to be with Nicky, no matter where she was or what she was doing. Nicky went to the bathroom, Emily followed her in. Nicky took off her bra, Emily watched her but didn't ask any questions. Later, when Nicky sat on the couch to think, Emily sat on the couch next to her.

"Can't I be by myself for a second?" Nicky asked.

"You're sad," Emily said.

"So?"

"I want to be with you."

"Why?"

Emily shrugged.

Nicky was exasperated. She wanted to think. If Emily weren't there, she'd go to her room and hide in the closet. But Emily was there.

"You want to know what's the matter?" Nicky said finally.

"Yes."

"I was humiliated at practice."

"What's that?"

Nicky considered this for a moment. "You know what it's like to be embarrassed?"

Emily nodded. "When I beep," she said.

Beep was Emily's word for passing gas. Nicky remembered when Emily had beeped in front of Nicky's friends. They had laughed at her, and Emily hadn't even known what she'd done that was so funny. Later, when Nicky had told her, Emily said she would be laughed at for the rest of her life because she couldn't stop the beeps.

"Yeah," Nicky said. "Being humiliated is ten

times worse than being embarrassed. It's like your feelings are hurt so badly, you can't stand it." Nicky picked at the hole in her jeans. She thought of Caitlin's note and began to pull harder at the hole.

"Do you want to go swing?" Emily asked. Swinging was her answer when she was sad or upset. When their pet gerbil died, Emily had gone out to the swing set every afternoon for a month.

"Why not?" Nicky said. She followed Emily out the back door, plopped onto the left swing, and started to pump. Higher and higher she flew, so high that she bounced slightly off the seat. Her stomach flipped over, and her head reeled.

She leaned her head back as she swung, and watched the ground rush toward her and then fall away, like a plane coming in for a landing, then changing course. She slowed and leaned back even farther so that her hair began to brush the ground. Back and forth, back and forth, slower and slower, she held on hard to the swing chains and felt the blood rush to her face. She shook her hair like a dog after a bath. How wonderful that it wasn't braided today!

How wonderful that her bra was up in her room.

How wonderful that she was playing with Emily, who didn't even know what a note was.

Part of her, Nicky suddenly thought, still liked to play with dolls and swing and be a little girl. Dolls were fun, playing with Jeannie was fun. Or used to be.

Suddenly, in mid-swing, she realized that Caitlin didn't know that Nicky had a Barbie.

She dragged her feet in the dirt and stopped. How could Caitlin have written that Nicky should give her bra to her Barbie when she didn't even know Nicky *had* a Barbie? Nicky had been careful never to let that information slip. Only Jeannie and Keescha knew about her Barbie.

Then Nicky remembered Jeannie's face the week before when Caitlin had called her immature. She remembered Jeannie saying, "Who said I was asking you to do anything?" on Monday on the bus when Nicky told her how dumb it had been mentioning dolls in front of Caitlin.

Caitlin hadn't written the note. Jeannie had.

She must have done it after they got off the bus. Maybe she had even *planted* it so Jeffrey would find it.

Nicky stared at the dirt and swallowed hard. For a moment, she couldn't catch her breath. Jeannie had swung harder than she ever had with a bat, and it felt as if she'd hit Nicky, her best friend, on purpose.

* * *

Nicky ate only a couple bites of her hamburger at dinner.

Later, she lay in the bathtub a long time, staring at the faucet, letting the warm water lap around her neck, and playing the terrible events of the day over and over in her head. Caitlin wasn't the enemy, Jeannie was.

When Nicky's father came into her room to tuck her into bed, Nicky wondered how much she should tell him. Was she too old to discuss all her problems with him? Caitlin's mother probably didn't tuck her in.

"Who are you playing tomorrow?" Mr. Durbin asked.

"The Fenders."

"Did you get all your homework done?"

"I didn't have any." Nicky worked the edge of her quilt between her fingers. Maybe she could tell him some of the problem, she decided, but not everything. And not cry her eyes out, either. "You know something, Dad?"

"What?"

"Tell me if this is weird or not."

"Okay." He smiled.

"I can act older, even if I don't feel that way all the time."

"What do you mean, honey?"

"I can act like these girls at school who wear lipstick and bras, but I can also play with dolls with Jeannie. Isn't that weird? It's like I'm a phony."

"You're not a phony," Mr. Durbin said. "You're growing up."

A knot tightened in Nicky's throat. "But, Dad — " She was going to say that part of her *didn't want to grow up* (at least not if growing up meant being like Caitlin), but she couldn't make herself say it.

"Different people grow up differently, Nicky. Everyone has to be allowed to say no if they're not ready."

"Some people don't know how to say no," Nicky said, thinking of Jeannie's note again. "At least they can't say it nicely."

"That is very true," Mr. Durbin said. His nostrils wiggled the way they did when he felt something deeply. The light from Nicky's nightstand reflected off his glasses, though, so Nicky couldn't see her father's eyes.

He waited, but Nicky couldn't think of anything else to say.

"That is very true," he repeated softly.

"Yeah." Nicky pulled her quilt up.

"Good night, sweetheart."

"Good night."

He kissed Nicky and left.

Nicky switched off the light. She thought about Jeannie writing that note and disguising her handwriting. Jeannie had meant to hurt her! She would probably want to play Barbies in high school! Jeannie was *such a baby*.

Then Nicky remembered her own feelings when Jeannie had asked her to play dolls in front of the other Daffodils. She hadn't said no very nicely then. Something inside her had snapped, had reacted instantly, had protected herself. NO, Nicky had said. Twice.

Maybe something inside Jeannie had snapped, too. She was protecting the part of her that wasn't ready to grow up.

As she lay there in the dark, Nicky couldn't see a way out for their friendship, though. What was she supposed to say? "Hey, Jeannie, it's okay that you wrote that mean note about me. I understand now that you just aren't ready to grow up."

Nicky rolled over and kicked at her quilt. It seemed as if all the Daffodils were going to be mad at one another, forever.

◇ 17 ◇
The Daffodil Bowl

"This is the last time I'm going to say it, Nicky," Caitlin said the next morning at school. "I didn't write that stupid note." They were standing outside the blue classroom door with the rest of the class, waiting for Mrs. Sirmyer.

"I know," Nicky said. Jeannie wasn't there yet.

Caitlin's mouth dropped open. "You do?"

"Yeah."

"Well, *who did, then?*"

"Yeah, who?" Jan and Erin chorused. Keescha didn't even look over. She leaned against the wall and picked at her fingernail.

"It doesn't matter," Nicky said.

"Well, it matters to *me*," Caitlin snapped. "Whoever it was set *me* up."

"What can you do about it now?" Nicky asked.

"Plenty." Caitlin narrowed her eyes. "I don't see why you're protecting the brat, whoever it is — "

Mrs. Sirmyer walked up at that moment, and Caitlin turned away.

Jeannie, it turned out, was absent. Nicky thought about her all day, wondering if she'd show up at the game.

Keescha ignored the entire fifth grade, including Nicky. She picked up a game of tetherball with a couple of girls from the sixth-grade class the first recess, and played kickball with some other sixth-graders at lunch and afternoon recess.

Caitlin, Erin, Jan, and Susan braided one another's hair during all three recesses.

Nicky wandered around. Whenever she looked at Caitlin, Caitlin was glaring at her. For the first time, Nicky wasn't looking forward to a Daffodil game.

That afternoon, Jeannie walked by Nicky without saying a word, then slipped onto the end of the bench.

◇ 121

Caitlin was unpacking equipment, but she saw this. Nicky watched her eyes slide back and forth, thinking. When she elbowed Jan and whispered something to her, Nicky knew Caitlin had figured it out.

"Hey, Nicky," Caitlin called. "I know who wrote that note about you!"

Jeannie looked up suddenly. Coach Kwock was unloading some boxes from her car in the parking lot.

"Yeah, *you*!" Caitlin looked right at Jeannie and laughed. "Look, Jan, her head popped right up!"

"But why would she write it?" Jan said. "She's supposed to be Nicky's best friend."

"Who knows?" Caitlin said. "That's probably why she wasn't at school today, too. She's chicken."

"I am not!" Jeannie said. "I hurt my knee. I tripped on the steps to our trailer."

"You weren't limping," sneered Caitlin.

"So?" Jeannie said. "It's better now. My mother just said to stay off of it this morning."

"Ha," Caitlin said. "What did you trip over, anyway? Your *Barbie*?"

Jeannie's small freckled face turned red, then her eyes filled with tears. Her jaw lost its squareness, began to buckle and finally to quiver.

"She's going to cry!" Caitlin sang out. "I can't believe it!"

Keescha had been throwing pitches to Taylor. Suddenly, she whirled around, her eyes narrowed. "You guys are so *screwed up*," she said. "That's what *I* can't believe. Boys at practice, makeup, bras — it's all so stupid! No wonder Jeannie, or *whoever*, did what she did."

Caitlin stepped toward Keescha, her chin thrust forward. "I don't know what your problem is, Keescha! Just because *you* don't want pretty things doesn't mean *we* don't. You're pitcher, but you don't own the team. Quit yelling at us!"

"You're the one who called Jeannie a baby and humiliated her," Keescha said to Caitlin. She looked directly at Caitlin's tie-dyed shirt. "And when I see stupid things, I call them stupid."

Nicky's face felt lopsided, half shocked, half sad. All of her was torn. No team captain could fix this mess, she thought. No team captain could make things like they used to be.

She looked at Jeannie, but Jeannie averted her eyes immediately. Taylor, Jan, and Erin looked away, too.

Coach Kwock jogged up to the team just then, glanced at her divided team, and scowled. "*Come on*, girls," she said sharply. A couple of strained moments passed, then she held up the bags of chips and soft drinks she was carrying. "Treats for everyone after the Daffodil Bowl, okay?" she said.

A few team members muttered thanks, and the coach assigned starting positions. The chilly fog of argument and accusation hung over the team, though.

No one said another word.

The Fenders were up to bat first. Nicky watched Jeannie jog out to right field. She was limping a little now, Nicky noticed. Maybe she really *had* hurt her knee, but Nicky knew that Jeannie could convince her mother to let her stay home for a scratch.

The field was still. The Daffodils stood stiffly in their positions, as if they were planted.

The first Fender walked up to the plate, and Keescha kicked at the dirt on the pitcher's mound. Nicky signaled a sidespin, then waited to pull down her bra, so as not to confuse Keescha.

Keescha nodded and threw the pitch across the plate. The batter connected, the ball burning past third base toward left field, low and hard like a golf ball. "Get it!" Keescha cried to Katie.

Katie put her mitt down, but missed. She scrambled after the ball and managed to heave it to second base so the runner stopped on first.

The Daffodils walked back to their positions and stared at one another.

The second Fender stepped up to the plate and cracked Keescha's pitch out over Taylor's head to Susan in center field.

Susan ran, stumbled, and flopped onto the ball after it bounced. She got up and threw the ball to Taylor, who fired it home so the Fender on third had to stop. "Nice throw, Taylor," Keescha said flatly. The rest of the team nodded, but they were still guarded and tight.

Suddenly, before the next batter came to the plate, Caitlin looked around at the team and blew the whistle. She stood with her feet on either side of first base, waiting until she had the attention of every Daffodil, and every Fender, as well. "Who's going to dent these Fenders in?" she cried.

The Daffodils all looked warily at one another and stayed planted where they were. Nicky could see what Caitlin was up to, though. She was trying to gather them all together.

Caitlin yelled again. "Who's going to dent these Fenders in?"

◇ 125

Still no Daffodil answered. They seemed unsure of what they were supposed to do.

Nicky pulled off her face mask. She took a deep breath. "The Daffodils!" she answered.

"*Who's going to dent these Fenders in?*" Caitlin cried.

"*The Daffodils!*" Nicky, and a few other players from the field, answered.

"WHO'S GOING TO DENT THESE FENDERS IN?" Caitlin cried one last time, punching her fist up.

"THE DAFFODILS!" The entire team now, including Keescha, cheered themselves. They jumped around and punched fists into gloves, getting loose, staying loose together.

"Play ball!" the umpire called.

Nicky pulled down her mask, squatted, and gave the two-finger-then-one-finger signal. Keescha pitched a perfect backspin, and the batter bunted it. Nicky tore off her face mask to get it, but Keescha had already scrambled for the ball and tossed it to Caitlin.

One away.

The next batter popped the ball up. Erin called "Mine!" and even though she missed it, everyone, including Keescha, said, "Good try." Nicky felt so relieved, she wanted to run out and hug every Daffodil.

Keescha struck out the next batter. "Way to go, Keescha," Erin sang out, and the inning was over.

Nicky ran with the rest of the Daffodils over to the bench and pulled off her mask and pads.

"It's a tougher league this year," Keescha said as she sipped from a water bottle and watched the Fender pitcher pitching to Taylor.

"That's true," Susan said. "I've never seen half those Fenders."

"Can I borrow your nail polish, Jan?" Erin asked. "I chipped a nail."

Keescha groaned. "Can't that wait?" she said.

"It isn't your business, Keescha," Caitlin said.

Nicky winced and waited for Keescha's retort, but Keescha ignored Caitlin. The Daffodils had warmed toward each other, but only for the game. Nicky suddenly realized that maybe this was all she could expect.

Just then, Renee cracked a ball out to right field.

"GO!" Keescha cried, leaping to her feet. "WAY TO BELT IT OUT THERE, RENEE!"

The team erupted, screaming, jumping, pounding one another, cheering Renee. From the edge of the mayhem, Nicky watched her teammates. She felt hushed and suddenly aware of herself, of her position watching, as if seeing a picture snapped at an unposed moment. The team had changed. It was a loss, a death of sorts, and like the time after her mother died, every connection would have to be made again. Nicky turned and jogged down to the end of the bench. "Jeannie?"

Jeannie didn't look up.

"Did you really hurt your knee?"

Jeannie snapped her head up. "Yes, I twisted it. I really did. It still hurts."

"I believe you. Come with me, okay?"

"Why?"

"You'll see."

They walked together to the school building. "Wait here," Nicky said. Jeannie sat down against a tree. "I'll be back in a second."

Jeannie looked puzzled, but Nicky just smiled. She ran into the restroom and took off her bra. When she came out, she had the bra wadded up in her fist and hidden behind her back. "To play in the game, you really should wear an ace bandage, right?"

Jeannie shrugged. "So?" she said.

"I've got the answer," Nicky said. "Pull up the leg of your jeans."

Jeannie did what she was told, then Nicky pulled out the bra and wrapped it around Jeannie's knee. The cups fit perfectly over the knee cap. "I can't think of a better use for this," she said.

"*Nicky!*" Jeannie said, giggling. Then she looked down at her bra bandage and was quiet for a moment. "I thought you'd never like me again," she said softly.

"I think I understand why you did it," Nicky said. "That helps."

"It seemed like you were becoming one of them," Jeannie said. "Like Caitlin, even though you said you didn't like Caitlin."

Nicky thought about that. She wasn't a Caitlin follower. She had supported Caitlin's rally out on the field, but she hadn't done it to win back the team or the captainship. She was growing up, and she, Nicole Durbin, didn't need a bra to do it. "All I know," Nicky said slowly, looking at Jeannie's knee, "is that this bra fits you better than it did me."

A sudden cry from the crowd at the softball field made them both look up. The Daffodils had scored, and Nicky saw her teammates — swirls of red and blue on last year's brilliant yellow. It was a new team color, a rainbow team of Daffodils, all growing and changing, and blooming in their own way, in their own good time.

About the Author

Christi Killien is the author of six novels for young adults and children, and a nonfiction book for adults called *Writing in a Convertible with the Top Down: A Unique Guide for Writers*. The American Library Association has named several of her books to its annual list of Recommended Books for the Reluctant Young Adult Reader, including *Putting on an Act*; *Rusty Fertlanger, Lady's Man*; and *Fickle Fever*. Ms. Killien lives in Seattle, Washington, with her husband and three children.

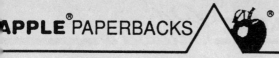

APPLE® PAPERBACKS

Pick an Apple and Polish Off Some Great Reading!

BEST-SELLING APPLE TITLES

❏ MT43944-8	**Afternoon of the Elves** Janet Taylor Lisle	$2.75
❏ MT43109-9	**Boys Are Yucko** Anna Grossnickle Hines	$2.95
❏ MT43473-X	**The Broccoli Tapes** Jan Slepian	$2.95
❏ MT40961-1	**Chocolate Covered Ants** Stephen Manes	$2.95
❏ MT45436-6	**Cousins** Virginia Hamilton	$2.95
❏ MT44036-5	**George Washington's Socks** Elvira Woodruff	$2.95
❏ MT45244-4	**Ghost Cadet** Elaine Marie Alphin	$2.95
❏ MT44351-8	**Help! I'm a Prisoner in the Library** Eth Clifford	$2.95
❏ MT43618-X	**Me and Katie (The Pest)** Ann M. Martin	$2.95
❏ MT43030-0	**Shoebag** Mary James	$2.95
❏ MT46075-7	**Sixth Grade Secrets** Louis Sachar	$2.95
❏ MT42882-9	**Sixth Grade Sleepover** Eve Bunting	$2.95
❏ MT41732-0	**Too Many Murphys** Colleen O'Shaughnessy McKenna	$2.95

Available wherever you buy books, or use this order form.

Scholastic Inc., P.O. Box 7502, 2931 East McCarty Street, Jefferson City, MO 65102

Please send me the books I have checked above. I am enclosing $_____ (please add $2.00 to cover shipping and handling). Send check or money order — no cash or C.O.D.s please.

Name_____ Birthdate_____

Address _____

City_____ State/Zip _____

Please allow four to six weeks for delivery. Offer good in the U.S.A. only. Sorry, mail orders are not available to residents of Canada. Prices subject to change.

APP693

APPLE Classics

❏ MA43389-X	**The Adventures of Huckleberry Finn**	Mark Twain	**$2.95**
❏ MA43352-0	**The Adventures of Tom Sawyer**	Mark Twain	**$2.95**
❏ MA42035-6	**Alice in Wonderland**	Lewis Carroll	**$2.95**
❏ MA44556-1	**Anne of Avonlea**	L.M. Montgomery	**$3.25**
❏ MA42243-X	**Anne of Green Gables**	L.M. Montgomery	**$2.95**
❏ MA43053-X	**Around the World in Eighty Days**	Jules Verne	**$2.95**
❏ MA42354-1	**Black Beauty**	Anna Sewell	**$3.25**
❏ MA44001-2	**The Call of the Wild**	Jack London	**$2.95**
❏ MA43527-2	**A Christmas Carol**	Charles Dickens	**$2.75**
❏ MA45169-3	**Dr. Jekyll & Mr. Hyde: And Other Stories** of the Supernatural	Robert Louis Stevenson	**$3.25**
❏ MA42046-1	**Heidi**	Johanna Spyri	**$3.25**
❏ MA44016-0	**The Invisible Man**	H.G. Wells	**$2.95**
❏ MA40719-8	**A Little Princess**	Frances Hodgson Burnett	**$3.25**
❏ MA41279-5	**Little Men**	Louisa May Alcott	**$3.25**
❏ MA43797-6	**Little Women**	Louisa May Alcott	**$3.25**
❏ MA44769-6	**Pollyanna**	Eleanor H. Porter	**$2.95**
❏ MA41343-0	**Rebecca of Sunnybrook Farm**	Kate Douglas Wiggin	**$3.25**
❏ MA45441-2	**Robin Hood of Sherwood Forest**	Ann McGovern	**$2.95**
❏ MA43285-0	**Robinson Crusoe**	Daniel Defoe	**$3.50**
❏ MA42323-1	**Sara Crewe**	Frances Hodgson Burnett	**$2.75**
❏ MA43346-6	**The Secret Garden**	Frances Hodgson Burnett	**$2.95**
❏ MA44014-4	**The Swiss Family Robinson**	Johann Wyss	**$3.25**
❏ MA42591-9	**White Fang**	Jack London	**$3.25**
❏ MA44774-2	**The Wind in the Willows**	Kenneth Grahame	**$2.95**
❏ MA44089-6	**The Wizard of Oz**	L. Frank Baum	**$2.95**

Available wherever you buy books, or use this order form.

Scholastic Inc., P.O. Box 7502, 2931 East McCarty Street, Jefferson City, MO 65102

Please send me the books I have checked above. I am enclosing $_____ (please add $2.00 to cover shipping and handling). Send check or money order — no cash or C.O.D.s please.

Name _____

Address _____

City _____ State/Zip _____

Please allow four to six weeks for delivery. Available in the U.S. only. Sorry, mail orders are not available to residents of Canada. Prices subject to change.

AC1092